"I'm not the kind ... *Julie. I wish I cou* ... *idea how much."*

"How did you become such an expert on what I need?"

"It's my job to understand people. I have to be able to read people, to understand their motivations, their personality types."

"And what's my personality type?"

"You're a nurturer. A natural healer. You take people who are hurting and broken and you try to fix them."

"And you don't want to be healed."

Ross bristled. "I'm not broken."

"Aren't you?"

Dear Reader,

Every once in a while a character comes along who just grabs me by the heart and doesn't let go. That's the way it was with Ross Fortune, the hero of *Fortune's Woman*. From the very first scene of the book, I adored Ross. He's this tough, no-nonsense private investigator on the outside, but inside he's a mass of contradictions. A man who loves his family deeply, who sacrificed much as a child and as a teenager to keep them together and to care for his siblings under difficult circumstances.

I knew someone very special needed to help him begin the process of healing the scars of his difficult childhood, and Julie Osterman seemed the ideal person. Julie has seen her share of pain. Unlike Ross, though, she hasn't withdrawn and kept the world at bay to protect herself. Instead, she reached out to help others, becoming a counselor to troubled youth.

These two seemed perfect for each other from the very beginning, and I loved writing their story!

All my best,

RaeAnne

FORTUNE'S WOMAN

RAEANNE THAYNE

Silhouette

SPECIAL EDITION®

Published by Silhouette Books

America's Publisher of Contemporary Romance

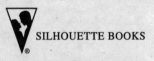

SILHOUETTE BOOKS

ISBN-13: 978-0-373-65452-9
ISBN-10:   0-373-65452-9

FORTUNE'S WOMAN

Recycling programs
for this product may
not exist in your area.

Visit Silhouette Books at www.eHarlequin.com

Printed in U.S.A.

Books by RaeAnne Thayne

Silhouette Special Edition

††*Light the Stars* #1748
††*Dancing in the Moonlight* #1755
††*Dalton's Undoing* #1764
***The Daddy Makeover* #1857
***His Second-Chance Family* #1874
§*A Merger...or Marriage?* #1903
***A Soldier's Secret* #1918
††*The Cowboy's Christmas Miracle* #1933
‡*Fortune's Woman* #1970

*Outlaw Hartes
†The Searchers
††The Cowboys of Cold Creek
**The Women of Brambleberry House
§The Wilder Family
‡Fortunes of Texas: Return to Red Rock

Silhouette Romantic Suspense

The Wrangler and the Runaway Mom #960
Saving Grace #995
Renegade Father #1062
**The Valentine Two-Step* #1133
**Taming Jesse James* #1139
**Cassidy Harte and the Comeback Kid* #1144
The Quiet Storm #1218
Freefall #1239
Nowhere to Hide #1264
†*Nothing to Lose* #1321
†*Never Too Late* #1364
The Interpreter #1380
High-Risk Affair #1448
Shelter from the Storm #1467
High-Stakes Honeymoon #1475

RAEANNE THAYNE

finds inspiration in the beautiful northern Utah mountains, where she lives with her husband and three children. Her books have won numerous honors, including two RITA® Award nominations from Romance Writers of America and a Career Achievement Award from *Romantic Times BOOKreviews* magazine. RaeAnne loves to hear from readers and can be reached through her Web site at www.raeannethayne.com.

Chapter One

What was the punk doing?

Ross Fortune stood beside a canvas awning–covered booth at the art fair of the Red Rock Spring Fling, keeping a careful eye on the rough-looking kid with the eyebrow bolt and the lip ring.

The kid seemed out of place in the booth full of framed Wild West art—photographs of steely-eyed cowboys lined up on a weathered fence, tow-headed toddlers wobbling in giant Tony Lamas, a trio of horses grazing against a stormy sky.

Yeah, he might be jumping to conclusions, but it didn't seem like the sort of artwork that would interest somebody who looked more wannabe rock star than cowboy, with his inky black hair, matching black jeans and T-shirt, and pale skin. But as Ross watched, the kid—who looked on the small side of maybe fourteen or fifteen—thumbed through the selection of unframed prints like they were the most fascinating things in the world.

Ross wouldn't have paid him any attention, except that for the past ten minutes he couldn't help noticing the kid as he moseyed from booth to booth in the gathering twilight, his eyes constantly shifting around. The punk seemed abnormally aware of where the artist-vendor of each booth stood at all times, tracking their movements under dark eyelashes.

Until the western photographs, he hadn't seemed much interested in whatever wares the artists were selling. Instead, he had all the tell-tale signs of somebody casing the place, looking for something easy to lift.

Okay, Ross was rushing to judgment. But something about the way the kid's gaze never stopped moving set all his alarm bells ringing. Even after the crowds started to abate as everybody headed toward the dance several hundred yards away, the kid continued ambling through the displays, as if he were searching for the perfect mark.

And suddenly he must have found it.

As Ross watched, the kid's gaze sharpened on a pink flowered bag somebody had carelessly left on a folding chair.

He moved to take a step forward, his own attention homing in on the boy, but just at that moment somebody jostled him.

"Sorry," muttered a dark-haired man in a Stetson who looked vaguely familiar. "I was looking for someone and wasn't watching where I was going."

"No problem," Ross answered. But when he looked back, the kid was gone—and so was the slouchy flowered bag.

Adrenaline pumped through him. Finally! Chasing a shoplifter was just what he needed right now.

He had been bored to tears all day and would have left

hours ago and headed back to San Antonio if he hadn't been volunteered by his family to help out on security detail for the Spring Fling, which was Red Rock's biggest party of the year.

At least now, maybe he might be able to have a little something to relieve the tedium of the day so he couldn't consider it a complete waste.

He stepped out of the booth and scanned the crowd. He saw his cousin J.R. helping Isabella Mendoza begin to pack away the wares at her textiles booth down the row a ways and he saw the Latino man in the Stetson who had bumped into him standing at a corner of a nearby water-color booth.

He also spied his despised brother-in-law, Lloyd Fredericks, skulking through the crowd, headed toward a section behind the tents and awnings, away from the public thoroughfare.

No doubt he was up to no good. If Ross wasn't on the hunt for a purse snatcher, he would have taken off after Lloyd, just for the small-minded pleasure of harassing the bastard a little.

He finally spotted the kid near a booth displaying colorful, froufrou dried-flower arrangements. He moved quietly into position behind him, his gaze unwavering.

This had always been his favorite moment when he had been a detective in San Antonio, before he left the job to become a private investigator. He loved that hot surge of energy before he took down a perp, that little thrill that he was about to tip the scales of justice firmly on the side of the victim.

He didn't speak until he was directly behind the boy. "Hey kid," he growled. "Nice purse."

The boy jumped like Ross had shoved a shiv between his ribs. He whirled around and shot him a defiant look out of dark eyes.

"I didn't do nothing. I was just grabbin' this for my friend."

"I'm sure. Come on. Hand it over."

The boy's grip tightened on the bag. "No way. She lost it so I told her I'd help her look for it and that's just what I'm doin'."

"I don't think so. Come on, give."

"You a cop?"

"Used to be." Until the politics and the inequities had become more than he could stomach. He didn't regret leaving the force. He enjoyed being a private investigator, picking his own cases and his own hours. The power of the badge sometimes had its privileges, though, he had to admit. Right now, he would have loved to be able to shove one into this little punk's face.

"If you ain't a cop, then I got nothin' to say to you. Back off."

The kid started to walk away but Ross grabbed his shoulder. "Afraid I'm not going anywhere. Hand over the bag."

The kid uttered a colorful curse and tried to break free. "You got it wrong, man. Let me go."

"Sure. No problem. That way you can just run through the crowd and lift a few more purses on your way through."

"I told you, I didn't steal nothin'. My friend couldn't remember where she left it. I told her I'd help her look for it so she could buy some more stuff."

"Sure kid. Whatever you say."

"I ain't lyin'!"

The boy wrestled to get free, and though he was small and slim, he was wiry and much more agile than Ross had given him credit for. To his chagrin, the teenager managed to break the grip on his arm and before Ross could scramble to grab him again, he had darted through the crowd.

Ross repeated the curse the kid had uttered earlier and headed after him. The punk might be fast but Ross had two major advantages—age and experience. He had chased enough desperate criminals through the grime and filth of San Antonio's worst neighborhoods to have no problem keeping up with one teenage boy carrying a bag that stood out like a flowery neon-pink beacon.

He caught up with him just before the boy would have slipped into the shadows on the edges of the art fair.

"Now you've pissed me off," Ross growled as he grabbed the kid again, this time in the unbreakable hold he should have used all along.

If he thought the boy's language was colorful before, that was nothing to the string of curses that erupted now.

"Yeah, yeah," Ross said with a tight grin. "I've heard it all before. I was a cop, remember?"

He knew he probably shouldn't be enjoying this so much. He was out of breath and working up a sweat, trying to keep the boy in place with one arm while he reached into his pocket with the other hand for the flex-cuffs he always carried. He had just fished them out and was starting to shackle the first wrist when a woman's raised voice distracted him.

"Hey! What do you think you're doing? Let go of him right this minute!"

He shifted his gaze from the boy to a woman with light brown hair approaching them—her eyes were wide and he briefly registered a particularly delectable mouth set in sharp, indignant lines.

He thought she looked vaguely familiar but that was nothing unusual in a small town like Red Rock, where everybody looked familiar. Though he didn't spend much time here and much preferred his life in San Antonio, the Fortune side of his family was among the town founders and leaders. Their ranch, the Double Crown, was a huge cattle spread not far from town.

The Spring Fling had become a large community event, and the entire proceeds from the art festival and dance went to benefit the Fortune Foundation, the organization created in memory of his mother's cousin Ryan, that helped disadvantaged young people.

Ross was a Fortune, and even though he was from the black-sheep side, he couldn't seem to escape certain familial obligations such as weddings and funerals.

Or Spring Flings.

He might not know the woman's name, but he knew her type. He could tell just by looking at her that she was the kind of busybody, do-gooder sort who couldn't resist sticking her lovely nose into things that were none of her business.

"Sorry. I can't let him go. I just caught the kid stealing a purse."

If anything, her pretty features tightened further. "That's ridiculous. He wasn't stealing anything! He was doing me a favor."

Despite her impassioned words, he wasn't releasing the boy, not for a moment. "I'm sure the Red Rock police over at the security trailer can sort it all out. That's where we're heading. You're welcome to come along."

He would be more than happy to let her be somebody else's problem.

"I'm telling you, he didn't do anything wrong."

"Then why did he run from me?"

The slippery kid wriggled more in his hold. "Because you wouldn't listen to me, man. I tried to tell you."

"This is my purse!" the woman exclaimed. "I couldn't remember where I left it so I asked Marcus to help me find it so I could purchase some earrings from a folk artist on the next row over."

Ross studied the pair of them, the boy so wild and belligerent and the soft, blue-eyed woman who looked fragile and feminine in comparison. "Why should I believe you? Maybe you're in on the heist with him. Makes a perfect cover, nice-looking woman working together with a rough kid like him."

She narrowed her gaze, apparently unimpressed with the theory. "I'll tell you why you should believe me. Because my wallet, which is inside the bag, has my driver's license and credit cards in it. If you would stop being so cynical and suspicious for five seconds, I can show them to you."

Okay, he should have thought of that. Maybe two years away from the job had softened him more than he wanted to admit. Still, he wasn't about to let down his guard long enough for her to prove him any more of a fool.

He tossed the purse at her. "Fine. Show me."

Her look would have scorched through metal. She scooped up the purse and pawed through it, then pulled out a brocade wallet, which she unsnapped with sharp, jerky movements and thrust at him.

Sure enough, there was a Texas driver's license with a pretty decent picture of her—a few years younger and with slightly longer hair, but it was definitely her.

Julie Osterman, the name read under her picture. He gazed at it for a full ten seconds before the name registered. He had seen it on an office door at the Foundation, next to his cousin Susan's. And he must have seen her there, as well, which explained why she looked slightly familiar.

"You work for the Fortune Foundation, don't you?"

"Yes. I'm a counselor," she tilted her head and looked more closely at him. "And you're Ross Fortune, aren't you?"

He should have recognized her. Any good cop—and private investigator—ought to be more tuned in to that sort of thing than the average citizen and be able to remember names and faces.

"I don't give a crap who you are," the wriggling teenager in his grip spat out. "Let go of me, man."

He was still holding onto the punk, he realized. Ross eased his grip a little but was reluctant to release him completely.

"Mr. Fortune, you can let go anytime now," Julie Osterman said. "It all happened exactly as he said. He was helping me find my purse, not stealing anything. Thank you so much for your help, Marcus! I'm so relieved you found it. You can go now."

Ross pulled his hand away, surrendering to the inevitable, and Marcus straightened his ratty T-shirt like it was two hundred dollars' worth of cashmere.

"Dude's a psycho," he said to no one in particular but with a fierce glare for Ross. "I tried to tell you, man. You should have listened. Stupid cop-pig."

"Marcus," Julie said. Though the word was calm enough, even Ross recognized the steel behind it.

Marcus didn't apologize, but he didn't offer more insults, either. "I got to fly. See you, Ms. O."

"Bye, Marcus."

He ambled away, exuding affronted attitude with every step.

When he was out of earshot, Julie Osterman turned back to him, her mouth set in those tight lines again. He was so busy wondering if she ever unbent enough to genuinely smile that he nearly missed her words.

"I hope you haven't just undone in five minutes here what has taken me weeks to build with Marcus."

It took him a few more seconds longer than it should have to realize she was wasn't just annoyed, she was fuming.

"What did I do?" he asked in genuine bewilderment.

"Marcus is one of my clients at the Foundation," she said. "He comes from, well, not an easy situation. The adults in his life have consistently betrayed him. He's never had anyone to count on. I've been trying to help him learn to trust me, to count on *me,* by demonstrating that I trust him in return."

"By throwing your purse out there as bait?"

"Marcus has a history of petty theft."

"Just the kind of kid I would send after my purse, then."

She fisted her hands on her hips and the movement made all her curves deliciously visible beneath her gauzy white shirt. "I wanted him to understand that when I look at him, I see beyond the mistakes he's made in the past to the bright future we're both trying to create for him."

It sounded like a bunch of hooey to him but he decided it might be wise to keep that particular opinion to himself right now, considering she looked like she wanted to skin him, inch by painful inch.

"Instead," she went on in that irritated voice, "you have probably just reinforced to a wounded child that all adults are suspicious and cynical, quick to judge and painfully slow to admit when they're wrong."

"Hey, wait a second here. I had no way of knowing you were trying for some mumbo-jumbo psychobabble experiment. All I saw was a punk lifting a purse. I couldn't just stand there and let him take it."

"Admit it," she snapped. "You jumped to conclusions because he looks a little rough around the edges."

Her hair was light brown, shot through with blond high-lights that gleamed in the last few minutes of twilight. With those brilliant blue eyes, high cheekbones and eminently kissable mouth, she was just about the prettiest woman he had seen in a long, long time. The kind of woman a man never got tired of looking at.

Too bad such a nice package had to be covering up one of those save-the-world types who always set his teeth on edge.

"I was a cop for twelve years, ma'am," he retorted. "When I see a kid taking a purse that obviously doesn't belong to him, yeah, I tend to jump to conclusions. That doesn't mean they're usually wrong conclusions."

"But sometimes they are," she doggedly insisted.

"In this case, I made a mistake. See, I'm man enough to admit it. I made a mistake," he repeated. "It happens to the best of us, even ex-cops. But I'm willing to bet, if you asked anybody else in the whole damn art fair, they would have reached the same conclusion."

"You don't know that."

He rolled his eyes. "You're right. I completely overreacted. The next time I see somebody stealing your purse, I'll be sure to just watch him walk on by."

The angry set of her features eased a little and after a moment, she sighed. "I hope I can convince Marcus you were just being an ex-cop."

Despite his own annoyance, he could see she genuinely cared about the boy. He supposed he could see things from her point of view. He had a particular soft spot for anybody who tried to help kids in need, even if they did tend to become zealots about it.

"I can try talking to the kid if that would help," he finally offered, though he wasn't quite sure what compelled him to make the suggestion. Maybe something to do with how her eyes softened when she talked about the punk.

"I appreciate that, but I don't think—"

A woman's frantic scream suddenly ripped through the evening, cutting off whatever Julie Osterman had intended to say.

Julie's heart jumped in her chest as another long scream echoed through the fair. She gasped and instinctively turned toward the source of the sound, somewhere out of their view, away from the public areas and the four long rows of vendor tents.

Before she could even draw a breath to exclaim over the noise, Ross Fortune was racing in the direction of the sound.

He was all cop now, she couldn't help thinking.

Hard and alert and dangerous.

She was too startled to do more than watch him rush toward the sound for a few seconds. It always managed to astound her when police officers and firefighters raced toward potentially hazardous situations while people like her stood frozen.

She knew a little about Ross Fortune from her friend Susan, his cousin. He had been a police officer in San Antonio but had left the force a few years ago to open his own private investigation company.

He was a trained detective, she reminded herself, and she would probably do wise to just let him, well, *detect.*

But as another scream ripped through the night, past the happy laughter of the carnival rides and the throbbing bass coming from the dance, Julie knew she had to follow him, whether she was comfortable with it or not.

Someone obviously needed help and she couldn't just stand idly by and do nothing.

Ross had a head start on her but she managed to nearly catch up as he darted around the corner of a display of pottery she had admired earlier in the evening.

Probably only ten seconds had elapsed from the instant they heard the first scream, but time seemed to stretch and elongate like the pulled taffy being sold on the midway alongside kettle corn, snow cones and cotton candy.

She ran after Ross and stumbled onto a strange, surreal scene. It was darker back here, away from the lights and noise of the Spring Fling crowd. But Julie could still tell instantly that the woman with the high-pitched scream was someone she recognized from seeing her around town, a blowsy blonde who usually favored miniscule halter tops and five-inch high heels.

She was staring at something a dozen yards away, illuminated by a lone vapor light, high on a power pole. A figure was lying motionless on the ground, faceup, and even from here, Julie could see a dark pool of what she assumed was blood around his head.

A third person stood over the body. It took Julie only a moment to recognize Frannie Fortune Fredericks, a frequent volunteer at the center.

And Ross's sister, she remembered with stunned dismay that she saw reflected in his features.

Frannie was staring at her hands. In the pale moonlight, they shone much darker than the rest of her skin.

"It's her. She killed him!" the other woman cried out stridently. "Can't you see? The bitch killed my Lloyd!"

Her Lloyd? As in Lloyd Fredericks, Frannie's husband? Julie looked closer at the figure on the ground. For the first time, she registered his sandy-blond hair and those handsome, slightly smarmy features, and realized she was indeed staring into the fixed, unblinking stare of Lloyd Fredericks.

This couldn't be happening...

Ross quickly crossed to Lloyd's body and knelt to search for a pulse. Julie knew even before he rose to his feet a moment later that he wouldn't have been able to find one. That sightless gaze said it all.

That was definitely Frannie's husband. And he was definitely dead.

Ross gripped his sister's arm and Julie noticed that he was careful not to touch her blood-covered hands. *How did he possibly have the sense to avoid contaminating evidence under such shocking circumstances?* she wondered.

"Frannie? What's going on? What happened?"

His sister's delicate features looked pale, almost bloodless, and she lifted stark eyes to him. "I don't... It's Lloyd, Ross."

"I can see it's Lloyd, honey. What happened to him?"

The screaming woman wobbled closer on her high heels. "She killed him. Look at her! She's got blood all over her. Oh, Lloyd, baby."

She began to wail as if her heart were being ripped out of her cosmetically enhanced chest. Julie would have liked to be a little sympathetic, but she didn't fail to notice the other woman only began the heartrending sobs when a crowd started to gather.

Ross turned to her. "Julie, do you have a phone? Can you call 911?"

"Of course," she answered. While she pulled her phone out of her pocket and started hitting buttons, she heard Ross take charge of the scene, ordering everybody to step back a couple dozen feet. In mere moments, it seemed the place was crawling with people.

The 911 operator had just answered when Julie saw a pair of police officers arrive. They must have been drawn to the commotion from other areas of the Spring Fling.

"This is Julie Osterman," she said to the 911 dispatcher. "I was going to report a…an incident at the Spring Fling but you all are already here."

"What sort of incident?" the dispatcher asked.

Julie was hesitant to use the word *murder,* but how could it be anything else? "I guess a suspicious death. But as I said, your officers are already here."

"Tell me what you know anyway."

The woman took what little information Julie could provide to relay to the officers, who were pushing the crowd even farther back.

When she hung up the phone with the dispatcher, she stood for a moment, not sure what to do, where to go. She disliked this sort of crowd scene, the almost avaricious hunger for information that seemed to seize people when something dramatic and shocking occurred nearby.

She wanted to slip away but it didn't feel quite right, especially when she had been one of the first ones on the scene. She supposed technically she was a witness, though she hadn't seen anything and knew nothing about what had happened.

Julie scanned the crowd, though she didn't know what she was seeking. A familiar face, perhaps, someone who could help her make sense of this shocking development.

In the distance, she saw someone in a black Stetson just on the other side of the edge of light emanating from the art fair. He made no move to come closer to investigate the commotion, which she found curious. But when she looked again, he was gone.

"Oh, Lloyd! My poor Lloyd."

The woman who had alerted them with her screams was nearly hysterical by now, standing just a few feet away from her and gathering more stares from the crowd. Julie watched her for a moment, then sighed and moved toward her.

Though she wanted to slap the woman silly for her hysterics—whether they were feigned or not—she supposed that wasn't a very compassionate attitude. She could at least try to calm her down a little. It was the decent thing to do.

She reached out and took the other woman's hand in hers. "Can I get you something? A drink of water, maybe?"

"Nooooo," she sobbed. "I just want my Lloyd."

Lloyd wasn't going to belong to anyone again—not his pale, stunned-looking wife and not this voluptuous woman who grieved so vociferously for him.

"I'm Julie," she said after a moment. "What's your name?"

"Crystal. Crystal Rivers. Well, that's not my real name."

"Oh. It's not?" she asked, with a perfectly straight face.

"It's my stage name. I'm a dancer. My real name is Christina. Christina Crosby."

"How about if I call you Chris?"

"Christy. That's what people call me."

Julie offered a smile, grateful that their conversation seemed to soothe the woman a bit—or at least distract her from the hysterics. "Okay, Christy. What happened? Can you tell me? All I know is that we heard you scream and came running and found him dead."

"I'll tell you what happened. She killed him. Frannie Fredericks killed my Lloyd."

Chapter Two

Julie frowned as the woman's bitter words seemed to ring through the night air.

She still couldn't quite believe it. She had always liked Frannie. The woman seemed to genuinely care about her volunteer work at the Foundation and she had always been friendly to Julie.

She supposed no one could really see inside the heart of someone else or know how they would respond when provoked, but Frannie had always seemed far too quiet and unassuming for Julie to accept that she had murdered her husband.

"How can you be so certain? Did you see her do it?"

"No. He was already dead when I came looking for him." She sniffled loudly and pulled a bedraggled tissue from her ample cleavage. "We were supposed to meet here and take off to my place after his obligations at the stupid Spring

Fling. He didn't even want to come, but Lloyd had business tonight he had to take care of."

Business at the Spring Fling? Who on earth tried to conduct business at a community celebration?

"What kind?" she asked.

"I don't know. Something important. Someone he had to talk to, he said. Maybe Frannie. Maybe he told her he was going to divorce her for me. I don't know. I just know she killed him. Now watch—her brother Ross and the rest of the Fortunes are going to cover it all up. They think they own this whole damn town."

Julie shifted, uncomfortable with the other woman's antagonism. She liked and respected all the Fortunes. Susan Fortune Eldridge was one of her closest friends and she adored Lily Fortune, who was the driving force behind the Fortune Foundation that had been founded in memory of her late husband.

"Ma'am? Are you the one who found the body?"

Julie turned and found Billy Addison, a Red Rock police officer with whom she had a slight acquaintance through the Foundation.

"I did," Crystal waved her scarlet red nails like she was rodeo royalty riding around the arena. "My poor Lloyd. Have you arrested Frannie Fredericks yet?"

"Um, not yet. Let's not jump the gun here, miss. We're going to be taking statements for some time now. I'm going to need to ask you a few questions."

"Anything. I'll tell you whatever you need to know. But I don't know why you need to ask anybody anything. It's plain as my nose job that Frannie did it. Look at her—she's got blood all over her."

She let out a dramatic sob, more for effect than out of any real emotion, Julie thought, with unaccustomed cynicism.

"Lloyd was going to leave her skinny butt," Crystal said. "She knew it and that must be why she killed him. That's what I was just saying."

"Do you know that for a fact, ma'am?" the officer asked her.

"I know they fought earlier today. On the phone. I was with Lloyd and I heard the terrible things she said to him. She called him a two-faced liar and a cheat and said as how she wasn't going to put up with it anymore."

"How did you hear her side of the conversation?" the officer asked. "Was she on speaker phone?"

Crystal gaped at him. "Um, maybe. I don't remember. Or maybe she was just talking real loud."

Or maybe the conversation never took place, Julie thought. She didn't know what to believe—but she did know she shouldn't be hearing any of this. Any affair between Lloyd Fredericks and Crystal Rivers was not something she wanted to know any more about.

She stepped away to leave the police officer to the interview. Still, Crystal wasn't exactly being unobtrusive. Her words carried to Julie as she walked through the crowd.

"I just know Frannie made my poor Lloyd's life a living hell. And now her brother's going to cover it up. Watch and see if the Fortunes don't all circle the wagons around her. You just watch and see."

The Fortunes *were* a powerful family in Red Rock. But most of the ones she had met through the Foundation were also decent, compassionate people who cared about the community and making it a better place.

The family also had its enemies, though—people who resented their wealth and power—and Julie had a feeling Crystal wouldn't be the only one who would whisper similar accusations about the Fortunes.

What a terrible way for the Spring Fling to end, she thought as she made her way through the crowd. The event should be a celebration, a chance for everyone in town to gather and help raise money for a worthy cause. Instead, one life had been snuffed out and several others would be changed forever, especially those in Lloyd's family.

Julie knew the Frederickses had a teenage son. Josh, she thought was his name. If she wasn't mistaken, he was friendly with Ricky Farraday Jamison, her boss Linda's son, even though Ricky was a few years younger than Josh.

Had anyone told him yet? she wondered. How terrible for him if he were somehow drawn to the scene by the commotion and the crowd and happened to see his father's body lying there. It was a definite possibility, even though the police were widening the perimeter of the scene, pushing the crowd still farther back.

Perhaps proactive measures were called for. Someone should find the boy first before he could witness such a terrible sight.

Ross Fortune seemed the logical person to find his nephew. She sighed. She really didn't want to talk to him. Their altercation seemed a lifetime ago, but she would still prefer not to have anything more to do with the man.

If she had her preference, she would escape this situation completely and go as far away as possible. It reminded her far too much of another tragic scene, of police lights flashing and yellow crime tape flipping in the wind and the hard, invasive stares of the rapacious crowd.

She had a sudden memory of that terrible day seven years earlier, driving home from work, completely oblivious to the scene she would find at her tidy little house, and the subsequent crime tape and the solemn-eyed police officers and the sudden terrible knowledge that her world had just changed forever.

She didn't think about that day often anymore, but this situation was entirely too familiar. Then again it would have been unusual if the similarities didn't shake loose those memories she tried to keep so carefully contained.

She didn't want Frannie's son to go through the same thing. He needed to be warned, whether she wanted to talk to his uncle again or not. She started through the crowd, keeping an eye out for the tall, gorgeous private investigator.

In the end, he found her.

"Julie! Ms. Osterman!"

She followed the sound of her name and discovered Ross in a nearby vendor booth with his sister and the Red Rock chief of police, Jimmy Caldwell.

Frannie Fortune was slumped in a chair while her brother hovered protectively over her. She looked exactly as Julie imagined *she* had looked that day seven years ago. Frannie's lovely, delicate features were stark and pale and her eyes looked dazed. Numb.

She wanted to hug her, to promise her that sometime in the future this terrible day would be just an awful memory.

"I told you, Jim," Ross said. "I was talking to Ms. Osterman just a row over when we heard a scream. We were the first ones on the scene, weren't we? Besides the other woman."

Julie nodded.

"You're the one who called 911, right?" the police chief asked her.

"Yes. But your officers were on the scene before I could even give the dispatcher any information. Probably only a moment or two after we arrived," she said.

The police chief wrote something in a notebook. "Can you

confirm the scene as you saw it? Lloyd was on the ground and Frannie was standing over him."

"Yes." She pointed. "And the other woman—Crystal—was standing over there screaming."

"You didn't see anyone else? Just Frannie and Crystal?"

Julie nodded. "That's right. Just them."

"Frannie? You want to tell me what happened before Ross and Ms. Osterman showed up?"

She lifted her shell-shocked gaze from her blood-stained pants to the police chief. "I don't know. I was looking for…I just…I found him that way. He was just lying there."

"Tell him, Frannie," Ross insisted. "Go ahead and tell Jim you had nothing to do with Lloyd's death."

"I…I didn't."

Jimmy scratched the nape of his neck. "That's not a very convincing claim of innocence, Frannie. Especially when you're the one standing here over your dead husband's body with blood on your hands."

Ross glared at him. "Frannie is not capable of murder. You have to know that. You're crazy if you think she could have done this."

The police chief raised a dark eyebrow that contrasted with his salt-and-pepper hair. "This might not be the best time for you to be calling names, Fortune."

"What else would you call it? My sister did not kill her husband, though she should have done it years ago."

"Appears to be no love lost between the two of you, was there?"

"I hated his miserable, two-timing guts."

"Maybe you need to be the one coming down to the station for questions instead of Frannie here."

"I'll go any place you want me to. But I didn't kill him any more than my sister did. I've got an alibi, remember? Ms. Osterman here."

"He's right. He was with me," she said.

"Lucky for you. Unfortunately, by the sound of it, Frannie doesn't have that kind of alibi. I'm going to have to ask you to come with me to the station to answer some questions, Frannie."

"Come on, Jimmy. You know she couldn't have done this."

"You want to know what I know? The evidence in front of me. That's it. That's what I have to go by, no matter what. You were a cop. You know that. And I'm also quite sure this is going to be a powder keg of a case. I can't afford to let people say I allowed the Fortunes to push me around. I have to follow every procedure to the letter, which means I'm going to have to take her in for questioning. I have no choice here."

Ross glowered at the man but before he could say anything, another officer approached them. He was vibrating with energy. Julie imagined in a quiet town like Red Rock, this sort of situation was the most excitement the small police force ever saw.

"We found what might be the murder weapon, sir," the fresh-faced officer said. "I knew you would want to know right away."

"Thanks, Paul," the chief tried to cut him off before he said more, but the officer didn't take the hint.

"It was shoved under a display table in one of the tents and it's got what appears to be blood on it. I'll have CSU process it the minute they show up. Take a look. What do you think, sir?"

All of them followed the man's pointing finger and Julie could see a large, solid-looking ceramic vase. When she turned back, she saw that Frannie Fredericks had turned even more pale, if that was possible.

"What's the matter?" Ross asked her.

She shook her head and looked back at her blood-stained slacks.

"Do you know anything about that vase?" Jimmy Caldwell asked her, his gray eyes intent on her features.

When Ross's sister clamped her lips together, the police chief leaned in closer. "You have to tell me, Frannie."

She suddenly looked trapped, her gaze flitting between Jimmy Caldwell and her brother.

"Fran?" Ross asked.

"It's mine. I bought it from Reynaldo Velasquez," she finally whispered. "I wanted to put it in the upstairs hallway."

Ross muttered an expletive. "Don't say anything else, Frannie. Not until I get you an attorney. Just keep your mouth shut, okay?"

She blinked at her brother. "Why do I need an attorney? I didn't do anything wrong. I just bought a vase."

"Just don't say anything."

"In that case," the police chief said, "I guess we'll have to continue this conversation at the police station."

"You don't have nearly enough to arrest her. You know you don't."

"Not yet." The police chief's voice was grim.

"Josh. You have to find Josh," Frannie said suddenly. She clutched her brother's arm. "Find him, Ross. Get him away from here."

He looked taken aback by her urgency. "I'll look for him."

"Thank you, Ross. You've always taken care of everything."

He opened his mouth to say something, then clamped it shut again.

"Let's go, Frannie," the police chief's voice wasn't unkind. "I'm sure it will be a relief to you to get away from this crowd."

"Yes," she murmured.

The police chief slipped a huge navy windbreaker over her blood-stained clothing, then wrapped his arm around her shoulders. By all appearances, it looked as if he were consoling the grieving widow but Julie saw the implacable set to his muscles, as if he expected the slight woman to make a break for it any moment.

Ross watched after them, his jaw tight. "This is a fricking nightmare," he growled. "Unbelievable."

"Do you need help finding your nephew? I was coming to find you and suggest you look for him. It would be terrible for him to stumble onto this scene without knowing the…the victim was his father."

He muttered an expletive. "You're right. I should have thought of that before. I should have gone to look for him right away."

"I'll help you," she said. "We can split up. You take the midway and I'll head to the dance."

He blinked at the offer. "Why would you want to do that? You've already been dragged far enough into this."

He wouldn't get any arguments from her on that score. She would much rather be home in her quiet, solitary house than wandering through a crowd looking for a boy whose world was about to change forever.

She shrugged. "You need help."

He eyes widened with astonishment, and she wondered why he found a simple offer of assistance so very shocking.

"Thanks, then," he mumbled.

"No problem. Do you have a picture of Josh?"

"A picture?"

"I can't find him if I don't know what he looks like," she pointed out gently.

"Oh right. Of course."

He pulled his wallet out of his back pocket, and she was more charmed than she had any right to be when he opened an accordion fold in the wallet and slid out a photograph of a smiling young man with dark-blond hair, brown eyes and handsome features.

"I'm almost certain I've seen him around at the Foundation but the picture will help immensely," she said. "I'll be careful with it."

"I have more," Ross answered.

"We should exchange cell phone numbers so we can contact each other if either of us finds him."

"Good idea," he said. He rattled off a number, which she quickly entered into her phone, then she gave him hers in return.

"Now that you mention cell phones, it occurs to me that I should have thought of that first," Ross said. "Let me try to reach Josh on his phone. Maybe I can track him down and meet him somewhere away from here."

She waited while he dialed, impatient at even a few more moments of delay. The longer they waited, the more likely Josh would accidentally stumble onto his father's body and the murder scene.

After a moment, Ross made a face and left a message on the boy's voice mail for him to call him as soon as possible.

"He's not answering. I guess we're back to the original plan. I'll cover the midway and you see if you can find him at the dance."

"Deal. I'll call you if I find him."

"Right back at you. And Ms. Osterman? Thank you."

She flashed him a quick smile, though even that seemed inappropriate under the circumstances. "Julie, please."

He nodded and they each took off in separate directions.

She quickly made her way to the dance, though she was forced to virtually ignore several acquaintances on her way, greeting them with only a wave instead of her usual conversation. She would have to explain later and hope they understood.

She expected Ross's call at any moment but to her dismay, her phone still hadn't rung by the time she reached the dance.

Country swing music throbbed from the speakers and the plank-covered dance floor was full. Finding Josh in this throng would be a challenge, especially when she knew him only from a photograph.

She scanned the crowd, looking for familiar faces. Finally, she found two girls she had worked with at the Foundation standing with a larger group.

"Hey, Ms. O." They greeted her with a warmth she found gratifying.

"Hey, Katie. Hi, Jo. I could use your help. I'm trying to find a boy."

"Aren't we all?" Jo said with a roll of eyes heavily framed in mascara.

Julie smiled. "A particular boy, actually. It's kind of serious. Do either of you know Josh Fredericks?"

"Sure," Katie answered promptly. "He's in my algebra class. He's kind of cute, even if he is super smart."

"Have you seen him lately? Tonight?"

"Yeah. It's weird. Usually he doesn't go two inches away from his girlfriend but I saw him by himself earlier, over by the refreshments. I think that was a while ago. Maybe an hour. He might have ditched the place by now."

"Thanks," she answered and headed in the direction they pointed.

She found Josh right where Katie had indicated, standing

near the refreshment table as if he were waiting for someone. She recognized him instantly from the picture Ross had provided. He was wearing a western-cut shirt and a black Stetson, just like half the other men here, and she could see his dark-blond hair and brown eyes like his uncle's.

She didn't know whether to feel relief or dismay at finding him. She did not want to have to explain to him why she was searching for him. She quickly texted Ross that she had located his nephew at the dance and waited close by, intending only to keep an eye on him until Ross arrived to handle things.

He looked upset, she thought after a moment of observing him. His color was high and he kept looking toward the door as if waiting for someone to arrive.

Did he already know about his father? No, she couldn't imagine it. Why would he linger here at the dance if he knew his father had just been killed?

After two or three minutes, Josh suddenly looked at his watch, then set down his cup on a nearby tray.

Rats. She was going to have to talk to him, she realized, as he started heading for the door. She waited until he walked out into the much cooler night air before she caught up to him.

"Are you Josh?"

He blinked a little, obviously startled to find a strange older woman talking to him. "Yeah," he said slowly, not bothering to conceal his wariness.

"My name is Julie Osterman. I work at the Fortune Foundation with your mother's cousin Susan."

"Okay." He took a sidestep away from her and she sighed.

"Josh, this is going to sound crazy, I know," she began, "but I need you to stay here for a minute."

"Why?"

She couldn't tell him his father was dead. That job should fall to someone closer to him, someone with whom he had a relationship. "Your uncle is looking for you," she finally answered. "He really needs to talk to you. If you can hang around here for a minute, he should be along any time now."

She hoped.

"What's going on?" His gaze sharpened. "Is it my mom?"

"Your mom isn't hurt. Ross can explain everything when he gets here?"

"No. Tell me now. Is it Lyndsey? She was supposed to meet me here but she never showed and she's not answering her phone. Is she hurt? What's going on?"

"Josh—"

"Tell me!"

She was scrambling for words when a deep male voice spoke from behind her.

"It's your dad, Josh."

Chapter Three

She turned with vast relief to see Ross walking toward them, looking tall and solid and certainly strong enough to help his nephew through this.

The boy's features hardened. "Did he hurt Mom again? If he did, I'll kill him this time, I swear. I warned him I would."

"You might not want to say that too loudly," Ross said grimly. "Your father is dead, Josh."

For all his bravado just seconds before, the teenager's color drained at the words.

"Dead? That's crazy." Even as he spoke, Julie thought she saw something flicker in his brown eyes, something furtive, secretive.

"It's true," Ross said. "I'm sorry, Josh."

The boy gazed at him blankly, as if he wasn't quite sure how to respond.

"What happened?"

Ross cleared his throat. "We don't know for sure yet."

"Did he have a heart attack or a stroke or something? Was he hit by a bus? What?"

Ross sighed. His gaze met Julie's for a moment and she saw indecision there as he must be weighing just how blunt he ought to be with his nephew.

She would have told him to be as honest as possible. Josh would find out all the gory details soon enough. In a town like Red Rock, the rumors would fly faster than crows on carrion. Better for him to hear the news from his family than for them to all dissemble about the situation, which he would probably find condescending and demeaning.

Ross must have reached the same conclusion. "It's too early to say anything with a hundred percent certainty but it looks like he was murdered."

"Murdered?" Josh blinked at both of them. "You're kidding me, right? This is all some kind of a sick joke. People in Red Rock don't get murdered!"

"I'm afraid it's no joke," Julie said, her voice soft with compassion.

"Who did it? Do they have any suspects?"

Ross's gaze met Julie's again with a wordless plea for help and she thought how surreal it was that just an hour ago they were wrangling over her purse, and now he was turning to her to help him through this delicate family situation.

It was hard enough telling Josh his father was dead. How were they supposed to tell Josh that his own mother was the prime suspect?

"They're still investigating," Ross said after a moment.

Josh pulled off his Stetson and raked a hand through his hair. "This is crazy. I can't believe it," he said again. "Where's my mom? How is she taking this?"

"Uh, that's the other thing I needed to talk to you about," Ross said.

Fear leapt into his dark eyes and he turned to Julie with an accusation in his eyes. "You said my mom wasn't hurt!"

"She's not," Ross assured him. "It's just…Frannie had to go to the police station to answer some questions."

Josh obviously wasn't a stupid boy. He quickly put the pieces together. "*Mom* had to go for questioning? They think *she* killed him?"

"Josh—"

The color that had leached away at the news of his father's death returned in a hot, angry flush. "That's the most ridiculous thing I've ever heard! If she had it in her to kill him, she would have done it years ago."

If Julie hadn't worked with troubled youth on a daily basis for the last five years, she might have found his bitterness shocking. Instead, she found it unutterably sad.

"They're only questioning her. She's not under arrest," Ross said. "I'm sure they'll figure out soon enough that your mom is innocent."

"What about his girlfriend? Are they questioning her? Or his last girlfriend? Or the one before that? I could give them a whole damn list of suspects!"

"I'm sure they'll question as many people as they can," Julie said. Unable to help herself, she laid a comforting hand on the boy's arm. Though by all appearances he despised his father, her heart ached at the pain she knew still waited for him down the road. Losing a parent was traumatic for anyone, no matter what their relationship.

Josh didn't flinch away from her touch, but he remained focused on his mother and her predicament.

"I should go to her," he said after a moment. "She's going to need me."

* * *

Ross couldn't seem to look away from that soft, comforting hand Julie placed on his nephew's arm. There was no good reason he could figure out that the sight should put a funny little ache in his chest.

He cleared his throat. "I promise, the police station is no place for you right now, Josh. You have to trust me on this."

He, however, needed to get his butt over there as soon as possible to find out what was happening with the investigation. He was torn between dueling obligations, one to his sister and one to his nephew during this difficult time.

"I'll be eighteen in two weeks, Uncle Ross. I'm not a child anymore."

"I know that. But I've spent most of my adult life in police stations and I can tell you the best place for you is at home. I'll go check on your mother."

"I want to see her."

"She won't be able to talk to you, son. Not if she's being questioned."

"Well, I can at least tell them that I know she couldn't have killed Lloyd," Josh answered.

His loyal defense of his mother struck a chord with Ross. It reminded him far too much of the way he used to stick up for Cindy, making excuses to the other kids when she would stay out all night drinking or would bring a new man around the house or, worse, would entirely forget about them all for a weekend binge.

The difference there was that he had foolishly been trying to protect an illusion, while Josh's efforts were on behalf of an innocent woman.

"Everything's going to be okay. Trust me. She's only being questioned. I'm sure she'll be home in a short time. Why don't you head on home and get some rest? You're going to have a lot to deal with in the coming days."

"I should be with her," Josh said stubbornly.

Julie again reached out to Josh and Ross saw that once more her quiet touch seemed to soothe him. "The absolute best way you can help your mother right now is to give her one less worry. You were the only thing she thought about as they were taking her in for questioning. She insisted that your uncle watch out for you and that's just what he's trying to do. As he said, you have to trust him right now to know what's best, okay?"

Her words seemed to resonate with Josh. He looked between the two of them and then sighed. "I guess."

Ross was astounded and more gratified than he wanted to admit that she would come to his defense like this, especially after their altercation earlier in the evening. That encounter and his own honest mistake over the purse had been a fortuitous meeting, he thought now. He didn't know what he would have done this evening without her.

The thought sparked an idea—a nervy one, sure, but one that would certainly lift a little of the burden from his shoulders.

"Josh, could you hang on here for a second while I talk to Ms. Osterman?"

His nephew looked confused but he nodded and Ross stepped a few paces away where they could speak in relative privacy.

"Look, I do need to get to the police station to see how things are going with Frannie, but I don't want to send Josh to his empty house alone. This is a huge favor to ask when I'm virtually a stranger to you and you've already done so much, but do you think you could stay with him for a while, while I check on my sister?"

As he might have expected, Julie's soft blue eyes widened with astonishment at the request. "But wouldn't you rather have someone in your family stay with him? Your cousin Susan, maybe?"

Susan would come in a heartbeat, he knew, and like Julie, she specialized in troubled adolescents. But he hated to ask the Fortune side of the family for anything. It was an irrational reaction, he knew, but for most of his life his particular branch of the family had always been the needy ones.

He didn't know how many times the Fortunes had bailed Cindy out of one scrape or another, before they had virtually cut ties with her out of frustration that nothing ever seemed to change.

Even though he loved and admired several members of his extended family, Ross preferred to handle things on his own when he could. And when he couldn't, he much preferred asking somebody who wasn't a Fortune for help.

"They're all going to be busy with the last few hours of the Spring Fling. Plus, now they're going to have to deal with damage control after Lloyd's murder."

It was bad public relations for the festival, especially since this was the second time a dead body had been found while the town celebrated. A few years earlier, an unidentified body turned up at the Spring Fling. The town had only just started to heal from that.

Her forehead furrowed for a moment and then she nodded. "In that case, of course. I'll be glad to stay with Josh as long as you need."

For one crazy moment, he longed to feel the soft comfort of her touch on *his* arm, though he knew that was ridiculous.

"Thanks a million. It won't be long. I'm sure I'll be taking Frannie home in just a few hours.

* * *

He had been far too optimistic, Ross thought an hour later as he stood in the Red Rock police chief's office.

"Come on, Jimmy. This is a mistake. You have to know that. There's no way on earth Frannie killed Lloyd."

"You were on the job long enough, you know how it works. We just want to talk to her but she's not saying a word. She's shutting us down in every direction. I have to tell you, that makes her look mighty guilty."

A white-coated lab tech pushed open the door. "Chief, I've got those results you put the rush order on."

"Excellent. You're going to have to excuse me, Ross. Why don't you go on home? There's nothing more you can do here tonight."

"I'll stick around. Somebody's going to need to drive Frannie home when you're done with this little farce here."

Jimmy opened his mouth to answer, then closed it again. "I can't make you leave. But if you really want to help your sister, tell her to cooperate with us. The quicker she gives us her side of the story, the quicker we can wrap this up."

Ross had been a cop for a long time, trained to catch subtle nuances in conversation. He didn't miss the way the police chief phrased his words. *Wrap this up* was a far cry from *send her home*.

Something about this whole thing gave him an ominous feeling. He suddenly guessed he was in for a long night.

Chapter Four

Four hours and counting.

From his perch in an empty detective's chair, Ross looked at the clock above the chief's glass-walled office in the Red Rock police station.

He couldn't think the long delay boded well for Frannie. It was now nearly half past midnight and she had been in an interrogation room for hours.

His poor sister. Eighteen years of marriage to Lloyd Fredericks had just about wrung every drop of spirit out of her. She must be sick over this ordeal.

What could be taking so long? Frannie should have been released hours ago. With every tick of the clock, his hopes for a quick resolution trickled a little further away.

When the police chief emerged from the hallway that housed the interview room and headed for his office, Ross rose quickly and intercepted him.

"What's going on, Jimmy? I need info here."

His friend gave him a long, solemn look and Ross's stomach suddenly clenched with nerves. He did not like the implications of that look.

"She's going to be charged, Ross. We have no choice."

He stared at the other man, not willing yet to accept the unthinkable. "Charged with what?"

The chief rolled his eyes. "With jaywalking. Lord, Ross, what the hell do you think, *with what*. With murder!"

This couldn't be happening. Ross balled his fists. "That's bull! This whole thing is bull and you know it! Frannie no more killed Lloyd than I did."

"Are you confessing?"

"I've thought about killing the bastard a thousand times," he answered the chief. "Does that count?"

"Sorry, but if we could prosecute thoughts, I doubt there would be anybody left *outside* the walls of my jail."

"What evidence can you possibly have against Frannie that's not circumstantial?" he asked.

The police chief just shook his head. "You know I can't talk about that, Ross, especially not with the suspect's own brother, even if he is an ex-cop and an old friend. Even if you weren't Frannie's brother, I couldn't tell you anything."

"Come on, throw me a little bone here. It's only been four hours since Lloyd's death. Why the big rush? You haven't even had time to look at any other possibilities! What about Crystal Rivers? She claimed she just stumbled onto the body and found Frannie there, but she doesn't exactly seem like the most upright, stalwart citizen of Red Rock. For all we know, she could have killed him, then waited around for somebody else to find him before circling back and throwing her big drama queen scene."

Jimmy was quiet for a moment, then he motioned toward his office. They walked in, and he shut the door and closed the louvered blinds to conceal their conversation from any other curious eyes that might be watching in the station house.

"Look, I don't know if this is my place, but you and I have been around the block together a few times, from our days at the academy together to our time in the same division in San Antonio. I respect you more than just about any detective on my force and you know I'd hire you here in an instant if you ever decided to come back to the job."

"I appreciate that. Just be straight with me, Jimmy."

"I'll just remind you who calls the shots around here when it comes to prosecutions. Bruce Gibson. That's not helping the situation for Frannie, especially when she's refusing to say anything about what happened."

Ross gazed at the other man as the implications sunk in. Bruce Gibson was the district attorney—and a particularly vindictive one at that. He was the one who chose when charges would be filed and what those charges would entail. Even if the police department wanted to pursue other leads, a district attorney could make the final choice about whether they had enough evidence to go forward with a prosecution.

And he had been one of Lloyd's closest friends, Ross suddenly remembered, had practically grown up at the Frederickses' mansion.

Gibson would be out for blood—and it would be a bonus to the man if he could extract a little of that blood from the Fortunes. Gibson had made no secret of the fact that he thought the Fortunes were too wealthy, too powerful. He was up for a tough re-election battle in the fall and from all appearances, he seemed to be making an issue of the fact that he considered himself a man of the people and wouldn't let somebody's social status sway prosecutorial decisions.

Added to that, there was no love lost between Ross and Bruce Gibson. Just a few weeks earlier, he and Ross had exchanged words over an incident involving a stable fire on the family ranch and the way the family was choosing to investigate it privately.

What a tangled mess. Any other district attorney would see how ludicrous this whole thing was.

"Can I see her?" he asked.

Caldwell gave him a long, appraising look, then finally nodded. "It's past normal visiting hours but we can make an exception in this case. It might take a few moments, though. She's in central booking."

Perhaps half an hour later, Ross was finally ushered by the young, fresh-faced police officer he had seen earlier on the murder scene to a stark white interview room. Frannie looked up when the door opened and Ross had to stop from clenching his fists again at the sight of her in a prison-orange jumpsuit.

Since his sister's ill-fated marriage to Fredericks years ago, he had seen her disheartened and hurt, he had seen her hopeless and bleak. But he didn't think he had ever seen her look so desperately afraid.

The chair scraped as he pulled it out to sit down and she flinched a little at the noise.

"Hey, Frannie-Banannie."

Her eyes filled up with tears at the childish nickname. "You haven't called me that in years."

He was suddenly sorry for that, sorry that while he had never completely withdrawn from his family, he had enjoyed the distance that came from living twenty miles away in San Antonio. He didn't have to be involved in the day-to-day drama of family affairs, didn't have to watch Frannie slowly become this washed-out version of herself.

"How are you doing, sis?"

She shrugged. "I guess you know they're charging me."

"Yeah. Jim told me. Sounds like Bruce Gibson is on the warpath."

Her mouth tightened but she only looked down at her hands.

"What happened, Frannie?"

"I don't want to talk about it."

"That's what I hear. But you told them you didn't do it, right?"

She didn't answer him. Instead she rubbed the fraying sleeve of the jumpsuit between her thumb and forefinger. "How's Josh?" she asked.

He sighed at her evasive tactic but decided to let it go for now. "He's fine. I sent him back to your house."

"He shouldn't be alone right now. Is someone with him?"

"Julie Osterman is with him."

"Julie? From the Foundation? Why?"

Because I didn't want to ask the family to bail us all out once again, he thought but could never say. "She was with me when…everything happened. I couldn't be in two places at once and I needed help and Julie seemed a good choice since she's a youth counselor and all, like Susan."

"Julie is nice."

Frannie sounded exhausted suddenly, emotionally and physically, and he wanted to gather her up and take care of her.

Those days were gone, though. Try as he might, he couldn't fix everything. He couldn't fix her marriage for the last eighteen years. He couldn't get his young, happy sister back. And he wasn't at all sure he could extricate her from this mess, though he sure as hell was going to try.

"Ross, I need you to do something for me."

"Anything. Whatever you need."

"Take care of Josh for me. Stay with him at the house. I know he's almost eighteen and almost an adult and will probably tell you he doesn't need anyone else but I don't want him on his own right now. Help him through this, okay? He's going to need you."

"Come on, Frannie. Don't worry. You'll be out before we know it and this will all be a memory."

"Just help him. You've always been far more of a father to him than…than Lloyd."

"You don't even need to ask, Fran. Of course I will."

"Thank you." She attempted such a forlorn smile it just about broke his heart. "I can always count on you."

If that were true, she wouldn't be in this calamity. She wouldn't have been married to Lloyd in the first place and she wouldn't be facing murder charges right now, if he had been able to rescue her from the situation years ago, like he'd wanted to.

"We'll get the best attorney we can find for you, okay? Just hang in."

She nodded, though it looked as if it took the last of her energy just to make that small gesture. He had a feeling in another minute, his baby sister was going to fold her arms on the interrogation room table, lay her head down and fall instantly asleep.

"Get some rest, okay?" he advised her. "Everything will seem better in the morning, I promise."

She managed another nod. Ross glanced at the officer who was monitoring the visit, then thought, to hell with this. He pulled his sister into his arms, noting not for the first time that she seemed as fragile and insubstantial as a stained-glass window.

"Thanks, Ross," she mumbled before the guard pulled her away and led her from the room.

The Spring Fling seemed another lifetime ago as Ross drove the streets of Red Rock toward the house where Frannie and Lloyd moved shortly after their marriage.

The security guard at the entrance to their exclusive gated community knew him. His fleshy features turned avid the moment Ross rolled down his window.

"Mr. Fortune. I guess you're here to stay with your sister's boy, huh? You been to the jail to see her?"

The news was probably spreading through town like stink in springtime. "Yeah. Can you let me in?"

"Oh, sure, sure," he said, though he made no move to raise the security arm. "Jail is just no place for a nice lady like Mrs. F. Why, you could have knocked me six ways to Sunday when my cousin Lou called to tell me what had happened at the Spring Fling. Too bad I was here working and missed everything."

Ross gestured to the gate. "Can you let me in, George? I really need to be with my nephew right now."

The guard hit the button with a disappointed kind of look.

"You tell Mrs. F. I'm thinking about her, okay?"

"I'll be sure to do that, George. Thanks."

He quickly rolled his window up and drove through the gate before George decided he wanted to chat a little more.

Lights blazed from every single window of the grand pink stucco McMansion he had always secretly thought of as a big, gaudy wedding cake. There was no trace of his sister's elegant good taste in the house. It was as if Lloyd had stamped out any trace of Frannie.

The interior of the house wasn't any more welcoming. It was cold and formal, white on white with gold accents.

Ross knew of two rooms in the house with a little personality. Josh's bedroom was a typical teenager's room with posters on the wall and clutter and mementos covering every surface.

The other was Frannie's small sitting room that hinted at the little sister he remembered. It was brightly decorated, with local handiworks, vivid textiles and many of Frannie's own photographs on the wall.

Lloyd had a habit of changing the security system all the time so Ross didn't even try to open the door. He rang the doorbell and a moment later, Julie Osterman opened the door, her soft, pretty features looking about as exhausted as Frannie's had been.

"I'm sorry I'm so late," he said. "I never expected things to take this long, that I would have to impose on you until the early hours of the morning."

"No problem." She held the door open for him and he moved past her into the formal foyer. "Josh tried to send me home and insisted he would be okay on his own, but I just didn't feel right about leaving him here alone, under the circumstances."

"I appreciate that."

"He's in the kitchen on the telephone to a friend."

"At this hour? Is it Lyndsey?"

Josh's young girlfriend had been a source of conflict between Josh and his parents, for reasons Ross didn't quite understand.

"I think so, but I can't be certain. I was trying not to eavesdrop."

"How is he?"

She frowned a little as she appeared to give his question serious consideration. Despite his own fatigue, Ross couldn't help noticing the way her mouth pursed a little when she was concentrating, and he had a wild urge to kiss away every line.

He definitely needed sleep if he was harboring inappropriate fantasies about a prickly busybody type like Julie Osterman.

"I can't really tell, to be honest with you," she answered. "I get the impression he's more upset about his mother being detained at the police station than he seems to be about his father's death. Or at least that appears to be where he's focusing his emotions right now. On the other hand, his reaction could just be displacement."

"Want to skip the mumbo jumbo?"

She made a face. "Sorry. I just meant maybe he's not ready—or doesn't want—to face the reality of his father's death right now, so it's easier to place his energy and emotion on his mother's situation."

"Or maybe he just happens to be more upset about Frannie than he is about Lloyd. The two of them didn't exactly get along."

"So I hear," she answered. "It sounds as if few people did get along with Lloyd Fredericks, besides Crystal and her sort."

"And there were plenty of those."

Her mouth tightened but she refrained from commenting on his bitterness. Lloyd's frequent affairs had been a great source of humiliation for Frannie. "How is your sister?" she asked instead.

"Holding up okay, under the circumstances."

"Do you expect them to keep her overnight for questioning, then?"

He sighed, angry all over again at the most recent turn of events. "Not for questioning. For arraignment. She's being charged."

Her eyes widened with astonishment, then quickly filled

with compassion. "Oh, poor Josh. This is going to be so hard on him."

"Yeah, it's a hell of a mess," he answered heavily. "So it looks like I'll be staying here for a while, until we can sort things out."

She touched him, just a quick, almost furtive brush of her hand on his arm, much as she had touched Josh earlier. Through his cotton shirt, he could feel the warmth of her skin and he was astonished at the urge to wrap his arms around her and pull her close and just lean on her for a moment.

"I'm so sorry, Ross."

He cleared his throat and told himself he was nothing but relieved when she pulled her hand away.

"Thanks again for everything you did tonight," he said. "I would have been in a real fix without you."

"I'm glad I could help in some small way."

She smiled gently and he was astonished at how that simple warm expression could ease the tightness in his chest enough that he could breathe just a little easier.

"It's late," she finally said. "Or early, I guess. I'd better go."

"Oh right. I'm sorry again you had to be here so long."

"I'd like to say goodbye to Josh before I leave, if it's all right with you," she said.

"Of course," he answered and followed her into the kitchen.

In his fantasy childhood, the kitchen was always the warmest room in the house, a place scattered with children's backpacks and clumsy art work on the refrigerator and homemade cookies cooling on a rack on the countertop.

He hadn't known anything like that, except at the occasional friend's house. To his regret, Frannie's kitchen wasn't anything like that image, either. It was as cool and formal as the rest of the house—white cabinets, white tile, stainless-steel appliances. It was like some kind of hospital lab rather than the center of a house.

Josh sat on a white bar stool, his cell phone up to his ear.

"I told you, Lyns," he was saying, "I don't have any more information than I did when we talked an hour ago. I haven't heard anything yet. I'll tell you as soon as I know anything, okay? Meantime, you have to get some rest. You know what—"

Ross wasn't sure what alerted the boy to their presence but before he could complete the sentence, he suddenly swiveled around to face them. Ross was almost certain he saw secrets flash in his nephew's eyes before his expression turned guarded again.

"Um, I've got to go, Lyns," he mumbled into the phone. "My uncle Ross just got here. Yeah. I'll call you later."

He ended the call, folded his phone and slid it into his pocket before he uncoiled his lanky frame from the chair.

"How's my mom? Is she with you?"

Ross sighed. "No. I'm sorry."

"How long can they hold her?"

"For now, as long as they want. She's being charged."

His features suffused with color. "Charged? With *murder?*"

Ross nodded, wishing he had other news to offer his nephew.

"This completely sucks."

That was one word for it, he supposed. A pretty accurate one. "Yeah, it does. But there's nothing we can do about it tonight. Meanwhile, Ms. Osterman needs to get on back to her house. She came in to tell you goodbye."

He was proud of the boy for reining in most of his outrage in order to be polite to Julie.

"Thank you for giving me a ride and staying here and everything," Josh said to her. "And even though I told you I didn't need you to stay so late, it was…nice not to be here by myself and all."

"You're very welcome." She smiled with that gentle warmth she just seemed to exude, paused for just a moment, then stepped forward and hugged the boy, who was a good six inches taller than she was.

"Call me if you need to talk, okay?" she said softly.

"Yeah, sure," he mumbled, though Ross was pretty sure Josh looked touched by her concern.

They both walked her to the door and watched her climb into her car. When she drove away, Ross shut the door to Frannie's wedding-cake house and wondered what the hell he was supposed to do next.

He would just have to figure it out, he supposed.

He didn't have any other choice.

This was just about the last place on earth he wanted to be right now.

In fact, given a choice between attending his despised brother-in-law's funeral and wading chest-deep in a manure pit out on the Double Crown, Ross figured he would much rather be standing in cow honey swatting flies away from his face than sitting here in this discreetly decorated funeral home, surrounded by the cloying smell of lilies and carnations and listening to all the weeping and wailing going on over a man most people in town had disliked.

It would be over soon. Already, the eulogies seemed to be dwindling. He could only feel relief. This all seemed the height of hypocrisy. He knew of at least a dozen people here who had openly told him at separate times over the last few days how much they had hated Lloyd. Yet here they were with their funeral game faces, all solemn and sad-eyed.

He glanced over at his nephew, who seemed to be watching the entire proceedings with an odd detachment, as if it was all some kind of mildly interesting play that had no direct bearing in his life.

Josh seemed to be holding up well under the strain of the last five days. Maybe too well. The boy's only intense emotion over anything seemed to be rage at the prosecuting attorney for moving ahead with charges against his mother.

It had been a hellish five days, culminating in this farce. First had come the medical examiner's report read at Frannie's arraignment that Lloyd had been killed with a blunt instrument whose general size and heft matched the large piece of pottery his sister had purchased shortly before the murder. Then reports had begun to trickle out that the heavy vase had several sets of unidentified fingerprints on it—and one very obvious identified set that belonged to his sister.

Added to Crystal's testimony that Lloyd had a heated phone call with Frannie shortly before the murder, things weren't looking good for his sister.

A good attorney with the typical cooperative client might have been able to successfully argue that Frannie's finger-prints would naturally be on the vase since she had purchased it just a short time earlier, and that a hearsay one-sided tele-phone exchange—no matter how heated—was not proof of murder.

But Frannie was not the typical cooperative client. Despite the high stakes, she refused to confirm or deny her involve-ment in Lloyd's murder and had chosen instead to remain mum about the entire evening, even to her attorney.

Ross didn't know what the hell she was doing. He had

visited twice more since the night of the murder in an effort to convince her to just tell him and the Red Rock police what had happened, but she had shut him out, too. Each time, he had ended up leaving more frustrated than ever.

As a result of her baffling, completely unexpected obstinacy, she had been charged with second-degree murder and bound over for trial. Even more aggravating, she had been denied bail. Bruce Gibson had argued in court that Frannie was a flight risk because of her wealthy family.

He apparently was laboring under two huge misconceptions: one, that Frannie would ever have it in her to run off and abandon her son and, two, that any of the Fortunes would willingly help her escape, no matter how much they might want to.

In the bail hearing, Bruce had been full of impassioned arguments about the Fortune wealth and power, the entire time with that smirk on his plastic features that Ross wanted to pound off of him.

The judge had apparently been gullible enough to buy into the myth—either that or he was another old golfing buddy of Lloyd's or his father, Cordell. Judge Wilkinson had agreed with Bruce and ordered Frannie held without bail, so now his delicate, fragile sister sat moldering in the county jail, awaiting trial on trumped-up charges that should never have been filed.

And while she was stuck there, he was forced to sit on this rickety little excuse for a chair, listening to a pack of lies about what a great guy Lloyd had been.

Ross didn't buy any of it. He had disliked the man from the day he married Frannie, when she was only eighteen. Even though she had tried to put on a bright face and play the role of a regular bride, Ross had sensed something in her eyes even then that seemed to indicate she wasn't thrilled about the marriage.

He had tried to talk her out of it but she wouldn't listen to him, probably because Cindy had pushed so hard for the marriage.

When Josh showed up several weeks shy of nine months later, Ross had put the pieces of the puzzle together and figured Lloyd had gotten her pregnant. Frannie was just the sort to try doing what she thought was the right thing for her child, even if it absolutely wasn't the right decision for *her.*

In the years since, he had watched her change from a luminous, vivacious girl to a quiet, subdued society matron. She always wore the right thing, said the right thing, but every ounce of joy seemed to have been sucked out of her.

And all because of Lloyd Fredericks, the man who apparently was heading for sainthood any day now, judging by the glowing eulogies delivered at his memorial service.

Ross wondered what all these fusty types would do if he stood up and spoke the truth, that Lloyd was just about the lousiest excuse for a human being he'd ever met—which was really quite a distinction, considering that as an ex-cop, he'd met more than his share.

In his experience, Lloyd was manipulative and dishonest. He cheated, he lied, he stole and, worse, he bullied anybody he considered weaker than himself.

Ross couldn't say any of that, though. He could only sit here and wait until this whole damn thing was over and he could take Josh home.

He glanced around at the crowd, wondering again at the most notable absence—next to Frannie's, of course. Cindy had opted not to come, and he couldn't help wondering where she might be. He would have expected his mother to be sitting right up there on the front row with Lloyd's parents. She loved nothing more than to be the center of attention, and what better place for that than at her son-in-law's memorial service, with all its drama and high emotion?

Cindy had adored her son-in-law, though Ross thought perhaps he'd seen hints that their relationship had cooled, since right around the time Cindy had been injured in a mysterious car accident.

Still, even if she and Lloyd had been openly feuding, which they weren't, he would have thought Cindy would come.

He was still wondering at her absence when the pastor finally wrapped things up a few moments later. With the autopsy completed, Lloyd's parents had elected to cremate his remains, so there would be no interment ceremony.

"Can we go now?" Josh asked him when other people started to file out of the funeral chapel.

Ross would have preferred nothing more than to hustle Josh away from all this artificiality. He knew people likely wanted to pay their respects to Lloyd's son, but he wasn't about to force the kid to stay if he didn't want to be there.

"Your call," he said.

"Let's go, then," Josh said. "I'm ready to get out of here."

As he had expected, at least a dozen people stopped them on their way to the door to wish Josh their condolences. Ross was immensely proud of his nephew for the quiet dignity with which he thanked them each for their sympathy without giving away his own feelings about his father.

They were almost to the door when Ross saw with dismay that Lloyd's mother, Jillian, was heading in their direction. Her Botox-smooth features looked ravaged just now, her eyes red and weepy. Still, fury seemed to push away the grief for now.

"How dare you show your face here!" she hissed to Ross when she was still several feet away.

Chapter Five

Several others at the funeral stopped to watch the unfolding drama and Ross did his best to edge them over to a quieter corner of the chapel, away from the greedy eyes of the crowd.

"My nephew just lost his father," he said calmly. "I'm here for him, Jillian. Surely you can understand that."

She made a scoffing sort of sound. "Your nephew lost his father because of *your sister!* If not for her, none of us would be here. He would still be alive. You have no right to come here. No right whatsoever. This service is for family members. For those of us who…who loved Lloyd. You never even liked him. You probably conspired with your sister to kill him, didn't you?"

It was such a ridiculous thing to say that Ross had no idea how to answer her grief-induced ravings.

"I'm here for Josh," he repeated. "Whatever you might think about my sister right now, and whatever the circumstances of Lloyd's death, Josh has lost his father. He asked me to come with him today and I couldn't let him down."

Though he *had* let him down, Ross thought. And he had let his sister down, over and over. He hadn't been able to get Frannie out of her lousy marriage. He had tried, dozens of times, until he finally gave up. But maybe he hadn't tried hard enough.

"I want you to leave. Right now." Jillian's features reddened and she looked on the verge of some apoplectic attack.

"We're just leaving, Grandmother," Josh assured her and Ross was proud of his nephew for his calm, sympathetic manner.

At that moment, Lloyd's father stepped up and slipped a supporting arm around his wife's shoulders. "That's not necessary. You don't have to leave, Joshua. Come along, Jillian. The Scofields were looking for you a moment ago."

Cordell gave Ross a quick, apologetic look, then steered his distraught wife away from them. Ross watched after him, his brow furrowed. He hadn't seen Lloyd's father in a few months but the man looked as if he had aged a decade or more. His features were lined and worn and he looked utterly exhausted.

Was all that from Lloyd's death? he wondered. He knew the Fredericks had always doted on their only son and of course his death was bound to hit them hard, but he hadn't expected Cordell to look so devastated.

Maybe Lloyd's death wasn't the only reason the man seemed to have aged overnight. Ross had been hearing rumors even before Lloyd's death that not all was rosy with the Fredericks' financial picture. He had heard a few whispers around town that Cordell and Lloyd had been late on some payments and had completely stopped making others.

It wouldn't have surprised him at all to learn that Lloyd

had been the one keeping Fredericks Financial afloat. Maybe Cordell was terrified the whole leaky ship would sink now that his son was dead.

He made a mental note to add a little digging into their financial records to the parallel investigation he had started conducting into Lloyd's death.

"Follow the money" had always been a pretty good creed when he'd been a cop and he saw no reason for this situation to be any different.

"Sorry about that, Uncle Ross," Josh said when they finally stepped outside into the warm afternoon, along with others who seemed eager to escape the oppressive funeral chapel. "Grandmother is…distraught."

Poor Josh had a bum deal when it came to grandparents. On the one side, he had Lloyd's stiff society parents. On the other, he had Cindy. She was no better a grandmother than she'd been a mother, alternating between bouts of spoiling her grandson outrageously with flamboyant gifts she couldn't afford, followed by long periods of time when she would ignore him completely.

"Don't worry about it," Ross assured him. "Jillian's reaction is completely understandable."

"It's not. She knows my mom. She's known her for eighteen years, since she married my dad. Grandmother has to know Mom would never kill him."

"It's a rough time right now for everyone, Josh."

"I don't care how upset she is. My mom is innocent! And then to imply that you were involved, as well. That's just crazy."

Ross sighed but before he could answer, he was surprised to see Julie Osterman slip outside through the doors of the chapel and head in their direction.

She wore a conservative blue jacket and skirt with a silky white shirt and had pulled her hair back into a loose updo, and she looked soft and lovely in the sunshine.

His heart had no business jumping around in his chest just at the sight of her. Ross scowled. It didn't seem right that she should be the single bright spot in what had been a dismal day.

How did she have such a calming presence about her? he wondered. Even some of Josh's tension seemed to ease out of him when she slipped her arm through his and gave a comforting squeeze.

"Hi, Ms. O."

She smiled at him, though it appeared rather solemn. "Hi, Josh. I was hoping to get a chance to talk to you."

"Oh?"

She studied him for a long moment. "I have a dilemma here. Maybe you can help me out. I promised myself I wasn't going to ask you something clichéd like how you're holding up. But then, if I don't ask, how am I supposed to find out how you're doing?"

Josh smiled, the first one Ross had seen on his features all day. "Go ahead and ask. I don't mind."

"All right. How are you doing, under the circumstances?"

He shrugged. "Okay, I guess. Under the circumstances."

"It was a lovely memorial service, as far as these things go."

"I guess." Josh looked down at the asphalt of the parking lot.

"When do you go back to school?" she asked.

"Tomorrow. I've got finals next week and I can't really miss any more school if I want to graduate with my class. Uncle Ross thinks I should study for finals at home."

He and Ross had argued about it several times, in fact. It was just about the only point of contention between them over the last five days.

"I just think he should take as much time as he needs," Ross said. "If he doesn't feel ready, he can probably take a few more days, as long as he gets the assignments from his teachers. There's also the scandal factor. Everybody's going to be talking about a murder at the Spring Fling and I want to make sure he's mentally prepared for that before he goes back to school."

"What do you think, Ms. O.?" Josh asked.

Ross could tell she didn't want to be dragged into the middle of things but Julie only smiled at both of them. "There are arguments to be made for both sides. But I think that you're the only one who can truly know when you're ready. As long as you feel prepared to handle whatever might come along, I'm sure returning to school tomorrow will be fine."

"I think I am," Josh answered. "But I won't know until I'm there, will I?"

Julie opened her mouth to answer but one of Lloyd's elderly aunts approached them before she could say anything.

"Joshua? I've been looking all over for you," she said. "You're not leaving already, are you?"

Josh slanted a look at Ross. "In a minute."

"You can't leave yet. Your great-grandmother is here. She specifically wanted to see you."

Josh looked less than thrilled about being forced to talk with more Fredericks relatives but he nodded and allowed himself to be led away by the other woman, leaving Ross alone with Julie.

"I didn't expect to see you here," he said after a moment.

He didn't add that if he had seen her earlier, it might have made the whole thing a little easier to endure.

She made a face. "I decided I would probably regret it if I didn't come to pay my respects. I know Jillian casually from some committees we've served on together and it seemed the polite thing to do, for her sake alone. But more than that, I wanted to come for Josh. It seemed…right, especially as I feel a little as if I were involved, since you and I were on the scene so quickly after it happened and I was with Josh for those few hours afterward."

"Makes sense. It was nice of you to come."

She studied him for a long moment. "Forgive me if I'm wrong, but I get the impression you're not very thrilled to be here."

His laugh was rough and humorless. "Is it that obvious? I can't wait to leave. We were just on our way out. And just so you don't think I'm rushing him away, Josh is as eager to get out of here as I am."

She frowned. "How is he really doing?"

He gazed toward the door, where Josh was talking politely to an ancient-looking woman in a wheelchair. "Not as peachy as he wants everybody to think. He isn't the same kid he was five days ago."

"That's normal and very much to be expected."

"I get the grieving process. I mean, even though his relationship with his dad wasn't the greatest, of course he's going to be upset that he died a violent death. But something else is going on. I can't quite put my finger on it."

One of the things Ross liked best about Julie Osterman was the way she gazed intently at him when he was speaking. Some women looked like they had their minds on a hundred other things when he talked to them, everything from what they had for breakfast to what they were going to say next. It bugged the heck out of him. But somehow he was certain Julie was focused only on his words.

"I'm sure he's also upset about his mother's arrest."

"True enough. If you want the truth, he acts like Frannie's arrest upsets him more than Lloyd's death. He's furious that his mother has been charged with the murder and that she's being held without bail."

"Have you talked to him about his feelings?"

He rolled his eyes. "I'm a guy, in case it escaped your attention."

"It hasn't," she murmured, an odd note in her voice that sent heat curling through him.

He cleared his throat. "I'm no good at the whole 'let's talk about our feelings' thing. Not that I haven't tried, though. Yesterday I took him out on my boat, thinking he might open up out on the water. Instead, we spent the entire afternoon without saying a word about his mom or about Lloyd or anything. Caught our limit between us, though."

Why he shared that, he wasn't sure and he regretted even opening his mouth. What kind of idiot thought a fishing trip might help a troubled teen? But Julie only gazed at him with admiration in the deep blue of her eyes.

"Brilliant idea. That was probably exactly what he needed, Ross. For things to be as normal as possible for a while. To do something he enjoys in a safe environment where he didn't feel pressured to talk about anything."

"I used to take my brothers when we were kids. I can't say we solved all the world's problems, but we always walked away from the river a little happier, anyway. Or at least we stopped fighting for a few minutes. And sometimes we even caught enough for a few nights' dinners, too."

She smiled at that, as he found he'd hoped she would. "You know, Ross, if you think it might help him cope with his grief, I would be happy to talk to Josh in a more formal capacity down at the Fortune Foundation."

He mulled the offer for a long moment, then he shrugged. "I don't know if he really needs all that."

"I'm not talking long-term psychotherapy here. Just a session or two of grief counseling, maybe, if he wants someone to talk to."

Ross thought of Josh's behavior since Lloyd's death. He had become much more secretive and he seemed to be bottling everything up deep inside. Every day since his father's murder, Josh seemed to become more and more tense and troubled, until Ross worried he would implode.

He had seen good cops take a long, hard journey to nowhere when they tucked everything down inside them. He didn't want to see the same thing happen to Josh.

His nephew wouldn't share what he was going through with Ross, but maybe a few sessions with Julie would help him sort through the tangle of his emotions a little better. He supposed it couldn't hurt.

"If he's willing, I guess there's a chance it might help him," he answered. "You sure you don't mind?"

"Not at all, Ross. I like Josh and I want to do anything I can to help him through this hard time in his life. I would say, from a professional standpoint, it's probably better if he gets some counseling earlier rather than later. Things won't become any easier for him the next few months, especially if the case against Frannie goes to trial."

"It won't," he vowed. He was working like crazy on his own investigation, trying to make sure that didn't happen. "I can't believe such a miscarriage of justice would be allowed to proceed."

"You were a police officer," she said. "You know that innocence doesn't always guarantee justice."

"True. But I'm not going to let my baby sister go to prison for something she didn't do. You can be damn sure of that."

Her mouth tilted into a soft smile that did crazy things to his insides. "Frannie is lucky to have you," she said softly.

He deliberately clamped down on the fierce urge to see if that mouth could possibly taste as sweet as his imagination conjured up.

"We'll see," he said, his voice a little rough. "If Josh is willing, when is a good time for me to bring him in?"

"I've got some time tomorrow afternoon, if that works. Around four, at my office?"

"I'll talk to Josh and let you know. I don't want to force him to do anything he's uncomfortable about."

"From the little I've learned about your nephew, I don't think you could force him to do anything he didn't want to do. I'm guessing it's a family trait."

He actually managed a smile, his first one in a long time. He was suddenly enormously grateful for her compassion and her insight. "True enough. Thank you for all your help. I've been baffled about what to do for him."

He didn't add that he felt as if was failing Josh, just as much as he had failed Frannie for the last eighteen years.

"You're doing fine," she answered. "Josh needs love most of all and it's obvious you have plenty of that to give him."

She touched his arm again, as he realized was her habit, and Ross felt the heat of it sing through his system.

He wanted to stay right here all afternoon, to just let her gentle touch soothe away all his ragged edges, all the tangles and turmoil he had been dealing with since Lloyd's murder and Frannie's arrest.

What was it about her that had such a powerful impact on him? She was lovely, yes. He had known lovely women before, though, and none of them exuded the same soft serenity that called to him with such seductive invitation.

"Sorry that took so long. We can leave anytime."

At Josh's approach, Julie quickly dropped her hand from his arm and Ross realized they had been standing there staring at each other for who knows how long.

Josh shifted his gaze between the two of them, as if trying to filter through the currents that must be zinging around.

"Um, no problem," Ross mumbled. "I guess we should go, then."

They said their goodbyes to Julie, and he couldn't help noticing that she looked as rattled as he felt, something that probably shouldn't suddenly make him feel so cheerful.

Julie studied the boy sprawled in the easy chair in her office.

For the past half hour, Josh had been telling her all the reasons he wasn't grieving for his father. He talked about Lloyd Fredericks as if he despised him, but then Julie would see flashes of pain appear out of nowhere in his eyes and she knew the truth of Josh's relationship with his father wasn't so easily defined.

"I'm not glad he's dead. I know I said that right after he was killed, but it's not true. I guess I didn't really want him dead, I just wanted him out of my life and my mom's life. It's weird that he's gone, you know? I keep expecting him to come slamming into the house and start picking on my mom for whatever thing bugged him most that day. Instead, it's only Ross there and he never says much of anything."

"It's natural for you to be conflicted, Josh. You're grieving for your father, or at least for the relationship you might have wanted to share with your father."

Josh shrugged. "I guess."

"Nobody can make that process any easier. We each have to walk our own path when it comes to learning to live with the things we can't have anymore. But one thing I've found that helps me when I'm sad is to focus not on the things that are missing in my life but instead on the many things I'm grateful to have."

"Glass-half-full kind of stuff, huh?"

"Exactly. You're in the middle of a crisis right now and many times it's hard to see beyond that. That's perfectly normal, Josh. But it can help ease a little of that turmoil to remember you've still got your uncle standing by your side. You've still got good friends who can help you through."

"I've got Lyndsey."

Josh had mentioned his girlfriend at least five or six times in their session. Julie hadn't met the girl but it was obvious Josh was enamored of her.

"You've got Lyndsey. Many people in your life care about you and are here to help you get through this."

"I know what I have. Just like I know what I have to protect."

Julie mulled over his statement, finding his choice of words a little unsettling.

"What do you need to protect? And from whom? Your mother? Lyndsey?"

He became inordinately fascinated with the upholstered buttons on the arm of the easy chair, tugging at the closest one. "The people I love. I should have acted sooner. I should have protected my mom from Lloyd a long time ago."

"How would you have done that? Your mother was a grown woman, making her own choices. What could you have done?"

After a long moment, he lifted his shoulders. "I don't know. I should have figured something out."

She pressed him on the point as much as she could before it became obvious he didn't want to talk anymore. He became more closed-mouthed and distant. Though they technically still had five minutes, she opted to end the session a little earlier.

"Thanks for…this," Josh said. "The talk and stuff. It helped a lot."

She had no idea what she had possibly been able to offer, but she smiled. "I'm glad. Will you come again?"

He hesitated just long enough to make the moment awkward. "I guess," he finally said. "I don't think I really need therapy or anything but I don't mind talking to you."

"Great."

She quickly wrote her cell number on a memo sheet from a dispenser on her desk. "I'm going to give you my mobile number. If you want to talk, I'm here, okay? Anytime."

"Even if I called you at three in the morning?"

She smiled a little at his cynicism, the natural adolescent desire to stretch every boundary to the limit. "Of course. I might be half asleep for a moment at first, but after I wake up a little, I'll be very happy you felt you could bother me at 3:00 a.m."

She wasn't sure he believed her, but at least he didn't openly argue.

Ross was thumbing through a magazine in the reception area when they opened Julie's office door. He rose to his feet and she was struck again by his height and the sheer solid strength of him.

With that tumble of dark hair brushing his collar and those deep brown eyes, he looked brooding and dark and dangerous, though she had come to see that was mostly illusion.

Mostly.

Her insides gave that funny little jolt they seemed to do whenever she saw him and she fought down a shiver. She had to get control of herself. Every time she was around the man, she forgot all the many reasons she shouldn't be attracted to him.

"Hey, Uncle Ross. I'm going to go see if Ricky is still shooting hoops out back," Josh said.

"Okay. I'll be out in a minute. I'd like to talk to Ms. Osterman."

Josh nodded, picked up his backpack and headed out the door. Josh had been her last appointment of the day and this was Susan's half day, so no other patients waited in the reception area.

She was suddenly acutely aware that she and Ross were alone and she ordered her nerves to settle.

"How did things go in there?" Ross asked.

She sent him a sidelong look as she closed and locked her office door. "Just fine. And that's all I can or will tell you."

"Did he tell you he insisted on going back to school today, over all my well-reasoned objections?"

"He did."

"Am I wrong in thinking he should take more time?"

She studied him, charmed despite all the warnings to herself by his earnest concern for his nephew's well-being. She knew Ross was trying to do the right thing for Josh and she could also tell by the note of uncertainty in his voice that he didn't feel up to the task.

She chose her words carefully, loath to give him any more reason to doubt himself. "I think Josh needs to set his own pace. He's supposed to graduate in two weeks. Right now it's important for him to go through the motions of regaining his life."

"He didn't say much about school today on the way over here, but I know it couldn't have been easy." His features seemed hard and tight for a moment. "I know how cruel kids can be, how they can talk, especially in small towns."

He spoke as if he had firsthand experience in such things and she had to wonder what cruelty he might have faced as a child. She wanted to ask, but she was quite certain he would brush off the question.

"Josh can handle the whispers around school," she answered. "He's a very strong young man."

"He shouldn't have to go through any of this," he muttered.

"But he does, unfortunately. Whether he should or shouldn't have to face it, this is his reality now."

"I wish I could make it easier for him."

"You are. Just by being there with him, caring for him, you're providing exactly what he needs right now."

He studied her for a long moment, a warm light in his brown eyes that sent those nerves ricocheting around her insides again. She wanted to stay right here in her reception area and just soak up that heat, but she knew it was far too dangerous. Her defenses were entirely too flimsy around Ross Fortune.

"Shall we go find Josh and Ricky?"

Could he hear that slight tremble in her voice? she wondered. Oh, she dearly hoped not.

"Right," he only said, and followed her outside into the warm May sunlight, where Josh was shooting baskets by himself on the hoop hanging in one corner of the parking lot of the Foundation.

"No Ricky?" Ross asked.

"Nope. He must have gone home while I was talking to Ms. O. Left the ball out here, though."

Josh shot a fifteen-foot jumper that swished cleanly through the basket.

"Wow. Great shot," Julie said.

"My turn," Ross said and Josh obliged by passing the ball to him. Ross dribbled a few times and went to the same spot on the half-court painted on the parking lot. He repeated Josh's shot, but his bounced off the rim.

Josh managed what was almost a smile. "Ha. You can never beat me at H-O-R-S-E. At least you haven't been able to in years."

"Never say never, kid." Heedless of his cowboy boots that weren't exactly intended for basketball, Ross rolled up the sleeves of his shirt. "Julie, you in?"

She laughed at the pair of them and the suddenly intent expression in two sets of eyes. "Do I look crazy? This appears to be a grudge match to me."

Her heart warmed when Josh grinned at her, looking very different from the troubled teen she knew him to be. "There's always room for one more."

"You'll wipe the parking lot with me, I'm sure. But why not?"

She decided not to tell them she was the youngest girl in a family of five with four fiercely competitive older brothers. Sometimes the only time she could get any of them to notice her was out on the driveway with the basketball standard her father had nailed above the garage door.

H-O-R-S-E had always been her favorite game and she loved outshooting her brothers, finding innovative shots they couldn't match in the game of elimination.

It had been years since she played basketball with any real intent, though, and she knew she would be more than a little rusty.

The next half hour would live forever in her memory, especially the deepening shock on both Ross's and Josh's features when she was able to keep up with them, shot for shot, in the first five rounds of play.

After five more rounds, Josh and Ross each had earned H and O by missing two shots apiece, while she was still hitting all her shots, despite the handicap of her three-inch heels.

"Just who's wiping the parking lot with whom here?" Ross grumbled. "I'm beginning to think we've been hustled."

"I never said I couldn't play," Julie said with a grin, hitting a one-handed layup. "There was no deception involved whatsoever."

She had to admit, she was having the time of her life. And Josh seemed much lighter of heart than he had been during their session. She still sensed secrets in him, but for a few moments he seemed to be able to set them aside to enjoy the game, which she considered a good sign.

After another half hour, things had evened out a little. She had missed an easy free throw and then a left hook shot that she secretly blamed on Ross for standing too close to her and blasting away all her powers of concentration. But she was still ahead after she pulled off a trick bounce shot that neither Josh nor Ross could emulate.

"I'm starving," Ross said. "What do you say we finish this another night?"

"You're just saying that because you know I'm going to win," Julie said with a taunting smile.

Ross returned it and she considered the game a victory all the way around, especially if it could help him be more light-hearted than she had seen him since they had found his brother-in-law's body.

"Hey, Julie, why don't you come to the house and have dinner with us?" Josh asked suddenly. "We could finish the game there after we eat."

"Dinner?" She glanced at Ross and saw he didn't look exactly thrilled at the invitation. "I don't know," she said slowly.

"Please, Julie. We'd love you to come," Josh pressed her. "You don't have other plans, do you?"

"Not tonight, no," she had to admit.

"Then why not come for dinner? Uncle Ross said he was going to barbecue steaks and there's always an extra we can throw on the grill."

"Well, that's a bit of a problem," she answered. "I'm afraid I'm not really much of a meat eater."

"Really?" Josh said with interest. "Lyndsey is a vegetarian."

"I wouldn't say I'm a vegetarian. I just don't eat a lot of red meat."

"Those are fighting words here in cattle country," Ross drawled.

She laughed. "I know. That's why you won't hear me saying them very loudly. I would prefer if the two of you would just keep it to yourselves."

"Okay, we won't blab your horrible dark secret to everyone—" Josh gave her a mischievous smile "—as long as you have dinner with us."

She was delighted that he felt comfortable enough to tease her. "That sounds suspiciously like blackmail, young man."

"Whatever it takes."

She returned his smile, then shifted her gaze to see Ross watching both of them out of those brown eyes of his that sometimes revealed nothing.

"I suppose we could throw something else on the grill for you," Ross said. "You eat much fish? We've still got bass from the other day."

If she were wise, she would tell Josh 'thanks but no thanks' for his kind invitation. She already felt too tightly entangled with Ross and his nephew. But the boy was reaching out to her. She couldn't just slap him down, especially if it might help her reach him better and help him through this grief.

"In that case, I would love to have dinner with you, as long as you let me pick up a salad and dessert from the deli on the way over."

"You don't have to do that," Ross said.

She smiled and tossed the basketball at him. "I don't mind. It's a weird rule in my family. The winner always buys the loser's dessert. You can consider the salad just a bonus."

He was still laughing as she climbed into her car and drove away.

Chapter Six

By the time she left the deli with her favorite tomato salad and a Boston cream pie, her stomach jumped with nerves and she could barely concentrate on the drive across town to the Fredericks' luxurious home.

She let out a breath. It was only dinner. This jittery reaction was absurd in the extreme. It was only a simple dinner with a client and his uncle.

Nothing more than that.

Still, she couldn't deny that Ross affected her more than any man had in recent memory. It had been seven years since her husband's death. Seven long, lonely years. She had dated occasionally since then but only on a casual basis. She knew she was the one who always put roadblocks up to avoid things becoming more serious. The time and the person never felt right.

For a long time, she had been too busy trying to glue

together the shattered pieces of her life. Then she had been too wrapped up in her new career as a child and family therapist and the new job at the Fortune Foundation to devote much time or energy to a relationship.

For the past year or so she had begun to think that she was finally in a good place to get serious about a man again, to try again at love. She had dated a few possibilities but nothing had ever come of them.

Ross Fortune was definitely not serious relationship material. Despite the attraction that simmered between them—and she knew she was not misreading those signs—Ross Fortune came with complications she wasn't prepared to deal with. Beyond his current family turmoil, she sensed he was a hard man, not very open to warmth and tenderness.

She tried to picture him being content spending a quiet evening at home with a child on his lap and couldn't quite manage it. But maybe she wasn't being fair to him. Maybe that restlessness she sensed was a result of his brother-in-law's murder and the subsequent fallout from it.

Julie sighed as she approached the Fredericks' large house that gleamed a pale coral in the fading sunlight. That unspoken attraction between them was real and intense, but for now that was all it could remain.

She wasn't sure she could afford to see what might come of it, not when she had the feeling Ross Fortune was the kind of man who could easily break her heart like a handful of twigs.

Josh, she reminded herself.

She was here only because he asked her, because she wanted to think they had formed a connection since his father's death and she wanted to help him sort through his jumbled mix of feelings.

Her own weren't important right now.

The evening was warm and pleasant as she closed her car door. In other neighborhoods, she might have heard the happy sounds of children playing in the last golden twilight hours before bedtime, but the Frederickses lived in Red Rock's most exclusive neighborhood. All she could manage to hear was the whir of air conditioners and a few well-mannered birds tweeting in the treetops.

Her own neighborhood near the elementary school was far different, an eclectic mix of old-timers who had lived in Red Rock forever and some of the new blood that had moved into the town, drawn by the quiet pace and friendly neighbors.

Moving here from Austin a year ago had been good for her, she thought as she rang the doorbell. She had made many new friends, she had a busy social life and she enjoyed a career where she felt she was affecting young lives.

Did she really need to snarl that up by yearning for a man who appeared unavailable?

At just that moment, Ross opened the door and she had to swallow hard. He was wearing Levi's and a navy-blue shirt with the sleeves rolled up. He looked casual and relaxed and her traitorous body responded instantly.

She was staring at his mouth. She realized it a half second too late and jerked her gaze up, only to find him watching her with a strange, glittery light in his eyes that struck her as vaguely predatory.

"Hi," she murmured.

"Evening."

"It's a gorgeous one, isn't it?"

He glanced past her to the soft twilight and blinked a little as if he hadn't noticed it before. "You're right. It is. Come in."

She followed him inside. Though his sister had been in

custody for less than a week, the grand house already felt a little neglected. A thin layer of dust covered the table in the foyer and several pairs of shoes were lined up by the door, something she was quite sure Frannie wouldn't have allowed.

"Where's Josh?" she asked.

"Holed up in his room, claiming homework. I'll let him know you're here in a minute. Actually, I'm glad to have a chance to talk to you alone first."

Her heart skipped a beat, despite her best efforts to control her reaction. "Oh?"

"About Josh, I mean."

She hoped he didn't notice her flushed features or the disappointment she told herself was ridiculous. "Of course."

"Do you mind coming out back with me? We can talk while I throw the steaks and your fish on the grill."

She nodded and followed him through the house, noticing a few more subtle signs of neglect in the house that weren't present when she was first here nearly a week ago. A few dirty dishes in the sink, a clutter of papers on the edge of the kitchen island, a jacket tossed casually over the back of a chair.

Ross grabbed a covered platter from the refrigerator, then opened the sliding doors to the vast patio that led to an elegantly landscaped pool. In the dusky light, the area looked quiet and restful. While she didn't much care for the style of the rest of the house, Julie very much admired the gardens around Lloyd and Frannie Fredericks' mansion.

She eased into a comfortable glider swing near the grill and watched while Ross transferred the meat from the plate to the grill with the ease of long practice. When he was done, he approached the swing and after a moment sat beside her, much to her dismay.

He was so big, so very masculine, and she was painfully aware of his proximity.

"What did you want to talk about?" she finally asked, hoping he didn't try prodding her again to reveal details about her counseling session with Josh earlier.

"I'm looking for an honest opinion here," he said. "What do you think about Josh's girlfriend?"

Okay, she hadn't been expecting that. "Lyndsey? I haven't met her."

"But Josh has mentioned her, right?"

"Yes. That first night when I stayed here with him while you were at the jail." She didn't want to breach Josh's confidences by mentioning all the times he had brought up her name during their therapy session. "Why do you ask? Don't you like her?"

Ross was quiet for a moment, a push of his boot sending the glider swaying slightly. "I've only met her briefly myself. Can't say whether I like her or not. But I know Frannie was concerned about how serious they seemed to be getting. Now that I've had a chance to take a closer look at the situation firsthand, I've got to admit, it worries me a little, too."

"In what way?"

"To me, it seems like they're together all the time. I mean, *all* the time! When he's not over at her place or she's not here, he's talking to her on the phone or texting her or talking to her online. I don't know how intense things were between them before Lloyd's death but I'm a little worried that he's becoming too wrapped up with her. He's only a kid, with his whole life ahead of him."

"Don't you remember your first love? They can be pretty intense."

"No," he said, his voice blunt. "I never had one."

She stared. "You never had a girlfriend?"

"No. Not in high school, anyway. I was too busy with… things."

"What kind of things? Sports?"

His mouth tightened. "Family stuff."

He didn't seem inclined to add any more, so Julie forced herself to clamp down on her curiosity to press him.

"Well, first love can be crazy for a teenager," she said instead. "Wonderful and terrible at the same time, full of raw emotions and all these fears and hopes and insecurities. I'm sure his emotional bond to Lyndsey is heightened by the chaos elsewhere in his life. She must seem like a sturdy rock he can hang on to."

"She strikes me as the clingy, needy sort, just from the little I've been able to see of her," Ross said.

She could barely think straight, sitting this close to him, but she did her best to rearrange her mind to gain a little clarity. "Well, that might be part of her appeal to him. Lyndsey is somebody who needs him. Look at things from Josh's perspective. His father is dead. His mother is in deep trouble, but not any kind of trouble he can solve for her. Aiding this girl with whatever troubles she's having might make Josh feel less helpless about the rest of the things going on in his world."

He pushed the swing again with his foot. "So you think I ought to let their little romance run its course?"

"Josh is almost eighteen. There's not really much you can do about it."

"I could lock him in his room and feed him only gruel," he muttered.

She laughed. "He's a teenage boy. I imagine he would figure out a way to sneak out and go for pizza."

He was quiet for a long moment. When she glanced over to gauge his expression and try to figure out what he was thinking about, she thought she detected a hint of color on his cheekbones.

"Should I take him to buy condoms, just to be on the safe side?" he asked, without looking at her.

The temperature between them seemed to heat up a dozen degrees and she knew it was not from the barbecue just a few feet away. She cleared her throat. "Maybe that's a conversation you ought to have with his mother."

"I can't discuss my nephew's sex life with my sister while she's in jail!"

She supposed she ought to be flattered that he felt he could discuss such a delicate subject with her, but she couldn't get past the trembling in her stomach just thinking about "Ross" and "condoms" in the same conversation.

"I can't tell you what to do," she said. "You're going to have to make that decision on your own. But I will say that if Josh were my son or in my care, it's certainly a conversation I would have with him, especially if he's becoming as serious with his girlfriend as you seem to believe."

He didn't look very thrilled by the prospect, but he nodded. "I guess I'll do that. Thanks for the advice. I can see why you make a good counselor. You're very easy to talk to."

She smiled. "You're welcome."

He gazed at her and she saw that heat flare in his eyes again. The world seemed to shiver to a stop and the night and the lovely gardens and the soft wind murmuring in the treetops seemed to disappear, leaving just the two of them alone with this powerful tug of attraction between them.

* * *

He was inches from kissing her.

Ross could feel the sweet warmth of her breath, could almost taste her on his mouth. He wanted her, with a fierce hunger that seemed to drive all common sense out of his head.

He tried to hang on to all the reasons he shouldn't kiss her. This was *not* supposed to be happening right now.

His life was in total chaos, he had far too many people depending on him and the last thing he needed was to find himself tangled up with someone like Julie Osterman, someone soft and generous and entirely too sweet for a man like him.

One kiss wouldn't hurt anything, though. Only a tiny little taste. He leaned forward and heard a seductive little catch of her breath, felt the brush of her breast against his arm as she shifted slightly closer.

His mouth was just a tantalizing inch away from hers when he suddenly heard the snick of the sliding door.

"Ross?" Josh called out.

Julie jerked away as if Ross had poked her with hot coals from the grill and the glider swayed crazily with the movement.

"Over here," Ross called.

He didn't like the way Josh skidded to a stop, his size-fourteen sneakers thudding against the tile patio, or the way his eyebrows climbed to find them sitting together so cozily on the glider.

He also didn't like the sudden speculative gleam in his nephew's eyes.

"Hi, Julie. I didn't hear you come in."

She was breathing just a hair too quickly, Ross thought.

"I only arrived a few moments ago. Your uncle and I were just…we were, um…"

"Julie was helping me with the steaks. And speaking of which, I'd better turn them before they're charred."

He definitely needed to get a grip on this attraction, he thought as he turned the steaks while Julie and Josh set the table out on the patio.

She was a nice woman who was doing him a huge favor by helping him figure out how to handle sudden, unexpected fatherhood. It would be a poor way to repay her by indulging his own whims when he had nothing to offer her in return.

"I think everything's ready," he said a few moments later.

"We're all set here," Julie said from the table, where she sat talking quietly with Josh about school. They had set out candles, he saw, and Frannie's nice china. It was a nice change from the paper plates he and Josh had been using while he was here.

He went inside for the russet potatoes he had thrown in the oven earlier while they were waiting for her to arrive, and he put the tomato salad Julie had brought into a bowl.

"Wow. I'm impressed," Julie exclaimed as he set the foil packet containing her fish on her plate and opened it for her. The smell of tarragon and lemon escaped.

"Better wait until you taste it before you say that," he warned her.

He knew only two ways to cook fish. Either battered and fried in tons of butter—something he tried not to do too often for obvious health reasons—or grilled in a packet with olive oil, lemon juice and a mix of easy spices.

He knew he shouldn't care so much what she thought but he still found it immensely gratifying when she closed her eyes with sheer delight at the first forkful. "Ross, this is delicious!"

He was becoming like one of the teens she worked with, desperate for her approval. "Glad you like it. How's the steak, Josh?"

His nephew was still studying the two of them with entirely too much interest. "It's good. Same as always."

"Nothing like family to deflate the old ego," Ross said with a wry smile.

"Sorry," Josh amended. "What I meant to say is this is absolutely the best steak I have ever tasted. Every bite melts in my mouth. I think I could eat this every single day for the rest of my life. Is that better?"

Julie laughed and it warmed Ross to see Josh flash her a quick grin before he turned back to his dinner. He didn't know what it was about her, but when she was around, Josh seemed far more relaxed. More like the kid he used to be.

"What are your plans after the summer?" she asked.

Josh shrugged. "I'm not sure right now."

Ross looked up from dressing his potato and frowned. "What do you mean, you're not sure? You've got an academic scholarship to A&M. It's all you could talk about a few weeks ago."

His nephew looked down at his plate. "Yeah, well, things have changed a little since a few weeks ago."

"And in a few *more* weeks, this is all going to seem like a bad dream."

"Is it?" Josh asked quietly and the patio suddenly simmered with tension.

"Yes. You'll see. These ridiculous charges against your mom will be dropped and everything will be back to normal."

"My dad will still be dead."

He had no answer to that stark truth. "You're not giving up a full-ride academic scholarship out of concern for your mother or some kind of misguided guilt over your dad's death."

Josh's color rose and he set his utensils down carefully on his plate. "It's my scholarship, Uncle Ross. If I want to give it up, nobody else can stop me. You keep forgetting I'm not a kid anymore. I'll be eighteen in a week, remember?"

"I haven't forgotten. But I also know that you have opportunities ahead of you and it would be a crime to waste those. I won't let you do it."

"Good luck trying to stop me, if that's what I decide to do," Josh snapped.

Ross opened his mouth to answer just as hotly but Josh's cell phone suddenly bleated a sappy little tune he recognized as being the one Josh had programmed to alert him to Lyndsey's endless phone calls.

He didn't know whether to be annoyed or grateful for the interruption. He had dealt with his own stubborn younger brothers enough to know that yelling wasn't going to accomplish anything but would make Josh dig in his heels.

"Hey," Josh said into the phone. He shifted his body away and pitched his voice several decibels lower. "No. Not the best right now."

Ross's gaze met Julie's and the memory of their conversation earlier—and all his worries—came flooding back. Was it possible Lyndsey was part of the reason Josh was considering giving up his scholarship?

Josh held the phone away from his ear. "Uncle Ross, I'm done with dinner. Do you care if I take this inside, in my room? A friend of mine needs some help with, um, trig homework. I might be a while and I wouldn't want to bore you two with a one-sided conversation."

He and Julie both knew that wasn't true. He wondered if he should call Josh on the lie, but he wasn't eager to add to the tension over college.

"Did you get enough to eat?"

Josh made a face. "Yeah, Mom."

Ross supposed that was just what he sounded like. Not that he had much experience with maternal solicitude. "I guess you can go."

The teen was gone before the words were even out of his mouth. Only after the sliding door closed behind him did Ross suddenly realize his nephew's defection left him alone with Julie.

"You know, lots of parents establish a no-call zone during the dinner hour," Julie said mildly.

He bristled for about ten seconds before he sighed. Hardly anybody had a cell phone twenty years ago, the last time he'd been responsible for a teenager. The whole internet, e-mail, cell phone thing presented entirely new challenges.

"Frannie always insisted he leave it in his room during dinner."

She opened her mouth to say something but quickly closed it again and returned her attention to her plate.

"What were you going to say?" he pressed.

"Nothing."

"You forget, I'm a trained investigator. I know when people are trying to hide things from me."

She gave him a sidelong look, then sighed. "Fine. But feel free to tell me to mind my own business."

"Believe me. I have no problem whatsoever telling people that."

She gave a slight smile, but quickly grew serious. "I was only thinking that a little more consistency with the house rules he's always known might be exactly what Josh needs right now. He's in complete turmoil. He's struggling with his mother's arrest and his father's death. Despite their uneasy relationship, Lloyd was his father and having a parent die isn't easy for anyone. Perhaps a little more constancy in his life will help him feel not quite as fragmented."

"So many things have been ripped from his world right now. It's all chaos. I was just trying to cut him a little slack."

She stood and began clearing the dishes away. "Believe it or not, a little slack might very well be the last thing he needs right now. Rules provide structure and order amid the chaos, Ross."

He could definitely understand that. He had craved that very structure in his younger days and had found it at the Academy. Police work, with its regulations and discipline—its paperwork and routine—had given him guidance and direction at a time he desperately needed some.

Maybe she was right. Maybe Josh craved those same things.

"Here, I'll take those," he said to Julie when she had filled a tray with the remains of their dinner.

After he carried the tray into the kitchen, he returned to the patio to find Julie standing on the edge of the tile, gazing up at the night sky.

It was a clear night, with a bright sprawl of stars. Ross joined her, wondering if he could remember the last time he had taken a chance to stargaze.

"Pretty night," he said, though all he could think about was the lovely woman standing beside him with her face lifted up to the moonlight.

"It is," she murmured. "I can't believe I sometimes get so wrapped up in my life that I forget to enjoy it."

They were quiet for a long time, both lost in their respective thoughts while the sweet scents from Frannie's garden swirled around them.

"Can I ask you something?" Ross finally asked.

If he hadn't been watching her so closely, he might have missed the slight wariness that crept into her expression. "Sure."

"How do you know all this stuff? About grieving and discipline and how to help a kid who's hurting?"

"I'm a trained youth counselor with a master's degree in social work and child and family development."

She was silent for a long moment, the only sound in the night the distant hoot of an owl and the wind sighing in the treetops. "Beyond that," she finally said softly, "I know what it is to be lost and hurting. I've been there."

Her words shivered through him, to the dark and quiet place he didn't like to acknowledge, that place where he was still ten years old, scared and alone and responsible for his three younger siblings yet again after Cindy ran off with a new boyfriend for a night that turned into another and then another.

He knew lost and hurting. He had been there plenty of times before, but it didn't make him any better at intuitively sensing what was best for Josh.

He pushed those memories aside. It was much easier to focus on the mystery of Julie Osterman than on the past he preferred to forget.

"What are your secrets?" he asked.

"You mean you haven't run a background check on me yet, detective?"

He laughed a little at her arch tone. "I didn't think about it until just this moment. Good idea, though." He studied her for a long moment in the moonlight, noting the color that had crept along the delicate planes of her cheekbones. "If I did, what would I find?"

"Nothing criminal, I can assure you."

"I don't suppose you would have been hired at the Foundation if you had that sort of past."

"Probably not."

"Then what?" He paused. "You lost someone close to you, didn't you?"

She gazed at the moon, sparkling on the swimming pool. "That's a rather obvious guess, detective."

"But true."

Her sigh stirred the air between them.

"Yes. True," she answered. "It's a long, sad story that I'm sure would bore you senseless within minutes."

"I have a pretty high bore quotient. I've been known to sit perfectly motionless on stakeouts for hours."

She glanced at him, then away again. "A simple background check would tell you this in five seconds but I suppose I'll go ahead and spare you the trouble. I lost my husband seven years ago. I'm a widow, detective."

Chapter Seven

For several moments, he could only stare at her, speechless.

She was a widow. He would never have guessed that, not in a million years, though he wasn't quite sure why he found the knowledge so astonishing—perhaps because she normally had such a sunny attitude for someone who must have lost her husband at a young age.

"I'm sorry. I shouldn't have pushed you to talk about something you obviously didn't want to discuss, especially after you've done nothing but help Josh and me."

"It's okay, Ross. I wouldn't have told you if I hadn't wanted you to know. I don't talk about it often, only because it was a really dark and difficult time in my past and I don't like to dwell on it. I prefer instead to enjoy the present and look ahead to the future. That's all."

"What happened?" he asked after a long moment.

He sensed it was something traumatic. That might help

explain her empathy and understanding of what Josh was dealing with. He braced himself for it but was completely unprepared for her quiet answer.

"He shot himself."

Ross stared, trying to make out her delicate features in the dim moonlight. "Was it a hunting accident?"

The noise she made couldn't be mistaken for a laugh. "No. It was no accident. Chris was…troubled. We were married for five years. The first two were wonderful. He was funny and smart and brilliantly creative. The kind of person who always seems to have a crowd around him.

"After those first two years, we bought a home in Austin," she went on. "I was working at a high school there and Chris was a photographer with an ad agency. Everything seemed so perfect. We were starting to talk about starting a family and then…everything started to change. *He* started to change."

"Drugs? Alcohol?"

"No. Nothing like that. He became moody and withdrawn at times and obsessively jealous, and then he would have periods where he would stay up for days at a time, would shoot roll after roll of film, of nothing really. The pattern on the sofa cushions, a single blade of grass. He once spent six hours straight trying to capture a doorknob in the perfect light. Eventually he was diagnosed as schizophrenic, with a little manic depression thrown in for added fun."

Ross frowned. He knew enough about mental illness to know it couldn't have been an easy road for either of them.

"You stayed with him?"

"He was my husband," she said simply. "I loved him."

"You must have been young."

"We married when I was twenty-four. I didn't feel young at the time but in retrospect, I was a baby. I suppose I must have been young enough, anyway, that I was certain I could fix anything."

"But you couldn't."

"Not this. It was bigger than either of us. That's still so hard for me to admit, even seven years later. For three years, he tried every possible combination of meds but nothing could keep the demons away for long. Finally Chris's condition started a downward spiral and no matter what we tried, we couldn't seem to slow the momentum. On his twenty-eighth birthday, he gave up the fight. He returned home early from work, set his camera on a tripod with an automatic timer, took out a Ruger he had bought illegally on the street a week earlier and shot himself in our bedroom."

Where Julie would be certain to find him, he realized grimly. Ross had seen enough self-inflicted gunshot wounds when he had been a cop to know exactly what kind of scene she must have walked into.

He knew her husband had been mentally ill and couldn't have been thinking clearly, but suddenly Ross was furious at the man for leaving behind such horror and anguish for his pretty, devoted young wife to remember the rest of her life. He hoped she could remember past that traumatic final scene and the three rough years preceding it to the few good ones they had together. "I'm so sorry, Julie."

He wanted to take it away, to make everything all better for her, but here was another person in his life whose pain he couldn't fix.

The unmistakable sincerity in Ross's voice warmed the small, frozen place inside Julie that would always grieve for the bright, creative light extinguished far too soon.

She lifted her gaze to his. "It was a terrible time in my life.

I can't lie about that. The grief was so huge and so awful, I wasn't sure I could survive it. But I endured by hanging on to the things I still had that mattered—my faith, my family, my friends. I also reminded myself every single day, both before his death and in those terrible dark days after, that Chris wasn't responsible for the choices he made. I know he loved me and wouldn't have chosen that course, if he could have seen any other choice in his tormented mind."

He didn't say anything for a long time and she couldn't help wondering what he was thinking.

"Is that why you work with troubled kids?" he finally asked, his voice low. "To make sure none of them feels like that's the only way out for them?"

She sighed. "I suppose that's part of it. I started out working on a suicide hotline in the evenings and realized I was making an impact. It helped me move outside myself at a time I desperately needed that and I discovered I was good at listening. So I left teaching and went back to school to earn a graduate degree."

"Do you miss teaching?" he asked.

"Sometimes. But when I was teaching six different classes, with thirty kids each, I didn't have the chance for the one-on-one interaction I have now. I can always go back to teaching if I want. I still might someday, if that seems the right direction for me. I haven't ruled anything out yet."

"Do you ever wonder if anything you do really makes a difference?"

How in the world had he become so cynical? she wondered. Was it his years as a police officer? Or something before then? It saddened her, whatever the cause.

"I have to give back somehow. I've always thought of it as trying to shine as much light as I can, even if it only illuminates my own path."

He gazed at her, his dark eyes intense, and she was suddenly painfully aware of him, the hard strength of his shoulders beside her, the slight curl of his hair brushing his collar.

"You're a remarkable woman," he said softly. "I'm not sure I've ever known anyone quite like you."

He wanted to kiss her. She sensed it clearly again, as she had earlier in the evening. She could see the desire kindle in his eyes, the intention there.

This time he wouldn't stop—and she didn't want him to. She wanted to know if his kiss could possibly be as good as she imagined it. Anticipation fluttered through her, like the soft, fragile wings of a butterfly, and she caught her breath as he moved closer, surrounding her with his heat and his strength.

The night seemed magical. The vast glitter of stars and the breeze murmuring through the trees and the sweet scents of his sister's flower garden. Everything combined to make this moment seem unreal.

She closed her eyes as his mouth found hers, her heart pounding, her breath caught in her throat. His kiss was gentle at first, as slow and easy as the little creek running through her yard on a hot August afternoon. She leaned into it, into him, wondering how it was possible for him to make her feel shattered with just a kiss.

She was vaguely aware of the slide of his arms around her, pulling her closer. She again had that vague sensation of being surrounded by him, encircled. It wasn't unpleasant. Far from it. She wanted to savor every moment, burn it all into her mind.

He deepened the kiss, his mouth a little more urgent. Some insistent warning voice in her head urged her to pull away and return to the safety of the other side of the patio, away from this temptation to lose her common sense—*herself*—but she decided to ignore it. Instead, she curled her arms around his neck and surrendered to the moment.

She had dated a few men in the seven years since Chris's suicide. A history teacher at the high school, a fellow grad student, an investment banker she met at the gym.

All of them had been perfectly nice, attractive men. So why hadn't their kisses made her blood churn, the lassitude seep into her muscles? She supposed it was a good thing he was supporting her weight with his arms around her because she wasn't at all sure she could stand on her own.

In seven years, she hadn't realized how truly much she had missed a man's touch until just this moment. Everything feminine inside her just seemed to give a deep, heartfelt sigh of welcome.

They kissed for a long time there in the moonlight. She learned the taste of him, of the wine they'd had with dinner and some sort of enticing mint and another essence she guessed was pure Ross. She learned his hair was soft and thick under her fingers and that he went a little crazy when she nipped gently on his bottom lip.

His tongue swept through her mouth, unfurling a wild hunger for more and she tightened her arms around him, her hands gripping him closely.

She didn't know how long the kiss lasted. It could have been hours, for all the awareness she had of time passing. She only knew that in Ross's arms, she felt safe and desirable, a heady combination.

They might have stayed there all night, but eventually some little spark of consciousness filtered through the soft hunger.

This was dangerous. Too dangerous. His nephew could come outside to the patio at any moment and discover them in a heated embrace.

Although Josh was almost eighteen, certainly old enough to understand about sexual attraction, she had a strong feeling Ross wouldn't be thrilled if his nephew caught them kissing.

She wasn't sure how, but she managed to summon the energy and sheer strength of will to pull her hands away and step back enough to allow room for her lungs to take in a full breath.

The kick of oxygen to her system pushed away some of the fuzzy, hormone-induced cobwebs in her brain but for perhaps an entire sixty seconds she could only stare at him, feeling raw and off balance. Her thoughts were a wild snarl in her head and she couldn't seem to untwist them.

An awkward silence seethed around them, replacing the seductive attraction with something taut and clumsy. She struggled for something to say but couldn't think of anything that didn't sound silly and girlish.

Ross was the first one to break the silence. "I swear, that wasn't on the agenda for the evening," he finally said.

His hair was a little tousled from her fingers and he looked rumpled and rough around the edges and rather dismayed at their kiss.

She found the entire package absolutely irresistible.

"I believe you."

"I'm not… I didn't intend—"

He raked a hand through his hair, messing it up even more. A muscle worked in his jaw and he seemed so uncomfortable that she finally took pity on him.

"Ross, don't worry. I'm not going to rush out and start looking at bridal books just because you kissed me."

His eyes widened with obvious panic at simply the word

"bridal." Under other circumstances, Julie might have laughed but it was all rather humiliating in the moment. She was still reeling from the most sensuous kiss she thought she had ever experienced and he just looked at her with that stunned, slightly dazed look, as if she had just stripped down and started pole dancing around the patio umbrella.

"If I could take back the last ten minutes, I would," he said.

She refused to acknowledge the sharp sting of his words. "Don't give it another thought."

"Like that's possible," he muttered.

At least the kiss left him just as off balance as it had her. She found some small comfort that he hadn't been completely unaffected by it, though she still wasn't thrilled that he seemed so aghast.

"Look," he said after another long, awkward moment. "I'm very attracted to you. I guess that's pretty obvious by now and I'd be lying if I tried to pretend otherwise. But this is not a really good time for me to be…distracted."

She wasn't sure she'd ever been called a distraction before and she didn't quite know how to react. At least he had prefaced it by admitting he was attracted to her.

"Right now my focus has to be my family," he said. "Frannie, Josh. They need me and I can't afford to let my attention be diverted by anything, especially not, well, something as complicated as a relationship."

Just because of his family? she wondered. Somehow she doubted it. While she was quite certain he wasn't using his difficult situation as an excuse, she had a feeling even if his family wasn't having such a hard time right now, Ross wouldn't be quick to jump into any involvement with her.

He struck her as a man who shied away from anything deeper or more meaningful than a quick fling.

"I understand," she murmured.

"Do you?" His eyes were murky with regret in the moonlight. Because he had kissed her? she wondered. Or because he was determined not to repeat it?

"You've been thrust into a tough role here with Josh, trying to do the right thing for him at the same time you're deeply worried about your sister. I can see why you want to keep the rest of your life as uncomplicated as possible."

He frowned, shoving his hands in his pockets. "Tell me I haven't jeopardized your willingness to help with Josh?"

She certainly wouldn't be able to quickly forget the magic and heat they had shared. But that didn't mean she couldn't move on from here.

"It was just a kiss, Ross! Of course I'm still willing to help with Josh, if he's interested in more sessions. That's a completely separate issue. I would still want to help him any way I could, even if you and I had just gotten naked and rolled around on the living room carpet for the last two hours."

She wasn't quite sure if it was her imagination but his eyes seemed to glaze slightly and he made a sound that might have been a groan. Julie regretted her flippancy. The last thing she needed right now was that particular image in her head, not with the unfulfilled desire still pulsing through her insides.

Ross drew in a ragged breath. "I'm glad for that, at least. Josh responds to you. I don't want to lose that because I overstepped."

She held a hand up. "Ross, stop. Let it go. It was just a kiss. Just a momentary impulse that doesn't mean anything. You're attracted to me, I'm attracted right back at you, obviously, but that's all it is."

To her amazement, he opened his mouth as if he wanted to disagree—which she decided would make Ross Fortune just about the most contrary man she had ever met, if he intended to argue both sides of the issue.

She decided not to put the matter to the test. "I'd better go," she said. "It's been a long day and I have paperwork to finish tonight."

He still looked as if he had more to say but he only nodded. "Thanks for coming. I'm sorry again that Josh ditched on you. I'll have a talk with him about keeping the cell phone away from the dinner table."

"Excellent idea."

"Let me just go call him down to say goodbye to you."

"That's really not necessary."

Right now she just wanted to leave so that she could try to put a little distance between them in an effort to regain both her dignity and a little perspective.

"It *is* necessary," he said. "Josh is the one who invited you to dinner with us and then he just abandoned you for a phone call, which I should never have let him get away with. The least he can do is come down to tell you goodbye."

She didn't want to argue, she only wanted to leave, but she decided to give in with good grace. He was right, Josh needed to hold onto civility and manners, even if his life had been turned upside down.

She waited in the ornate foyer of the Frederickses' home while Ross hurried up the stairs to his nephew's room. A moment later, he returned with Josh, who rubbed the back of his neck and looked embarrassed.

"Sorry about leaving, Julie. It was way rude of me and I shouldn't have done it. I wasn't thinking about what bad manners it was, I was just... I needed to talk to my friend."

"I understand. Next time, maybe you could wait until we've all finished eating to take your phone call."

"I'll try to remember to do that. Thanks for coming to dinner and for…everything else today."

"You're welcome. I enjoyed it." *Some parts more than others,* she added silently to herself, and she forced herself not to look at Ross even as she felt a blush steal over her cheeks.

"We never did get to finish playing H-O-R-S-E."

"We'll have to schedule a rematch next time we have a session. If you think you want another one, anyway."

He shrugged. "I guess. You're pretty easy to talk to."

"Thanks." She smiled. "How about Tuesday after school?"

"That should work, I think."

"I'll see you then. Be sure to bring your game for afterward. You wouldn't want me to whip your butt on the court again."

He laughed. "I'll see if I can find it," he said. "See you later."

He headed up the stairs again, leaving her alone with Ross. He looked rough-edged and darkly handsome amid the pale, elegant furnishings of the house and she had a tough time not stepping forward and tasting that hard mouth one last time.

"Thanks again for dinner, Ross," she forced herself to say. "It was delicious."

"You're welcome."

They exchanged one more awkward, tentative smile, then she opened the door and walked out into the Texas night.

As she hurried to her car, she couldn't help wondering how one kiss had managed to sear away seven years of restraint.

Ross stood on his sister's veranda and watched Julie drive away in a sensible silver sedan.

He still felt as if he'd been tied feetfirst to the back end of a mule and dragged through cactus for a few dozen miles.

That kiss. Damn it, he didn't need this right now. He had never known anything like it, that wild fire in his blood that still seemed to sizzle and burn.

He had wanted to make love to her, right there on Frannie's Italian tile patio table. Even now, he could remember the sweet, luscious taste of her, the smell of her, like juicy peaches ripened by the sun that he couldn't wait to sink his teeth into.

What was he supposed to do with a woman like Julie Osterman? She was far too sweet, far too centered for someone like him.

She had lost a husband.

Just thinking about it made his heart ache. He could picture her—younger, even more idealistic, certain she could fix everything wrong in the world. And then to come up against such a tough, thorny thing as mental illness in someone she loved. It would have broken a woman who wasn't as strong as Julie.

She was a lovely, courageous, compassionate woman.

And not for him.

Ross gazed out at the night. What the hell did a man like him have to offer someone like her? She needed softness, romance, tenderness, especially after the pain she had been forced to endure.

He didn't know if he was capable of any of those things. He was cynical and rough, more used to frozen pizza than candlelight dinners. He liked his life on his own and wasn't sure he had room inside it for a woman like Julie.

He couldn't let himself kiss her again, especially not after he'd told her what a mistake it had been. As much as he might want to hold her in his arms, it wouldn't be fair to her to give her any ideas that he might be open to starting something with her, not when he would only end up hurting and disillusioning her.

Like he did everybody else.

He let out a breath, wishing for a good, stiff drink. He needed something to push back the regret that he wouldn't have the chance to taste that delectable mouth again, to hear her soft little sigh of arousal, to feel her curves pressing against him. Frannie and Lloyd had a well-stocked liquor cabinet but he wasn't sure it was a good idea for Josh to see him turning to alcohol to escape the weight of his obligations.

He heard the creak of the door behind him and Ross turned to see his nephew standing in the lighted doorway, studying him with concern in his eyes.

"Everything okay?" Josh asked.

"Sure. Why wouldn't it be?"

His nephew shrugged. "I don't know. You've just been standing out here without moving for at least half an hour. My bedroom window has a perfect view of the front door and I watched you while I was on the phone."

"Oh, right. Your study session."

Josh flashed him a quick, rueful grin but it faded quickly and those secrets took its place. He definitely needed to figure out what was going on with the kid.

"So what's up?" Josh asked. "Is something wrong?"

"No. I was just…thinking."

"About my dad's murder and the case against my mom?"

That was exactly what he *should* have been thinking about out here. The boy's words were a harsh reminder of yet another reason he needed to stay away from Julie—the most important one.

She distracted him at a time when he could least afford the inattention. He had a job to do—clearing his sister. It was quite possibly the most important case of his career, the one he had the most stake in, and he needed to focus.

"There are still a lot of inconsistencies," Ross said instead of answering his nephew directly. "The whole thing is making me crazy, if you want to know the truth. If your mom would only try to defend herself, things would go much easier for her. We just need to hear her side of the story."

Josh leaned against the pillar, his arms crossed over his chest. "Why do you think she's not talking?"

The question was just a little too casual. He searched Josh's features but his face was in shadows and Ross couldn't quite read him.

"It's a good question," he said. "One I sure wish I could answer. Why do *you* think she's staying quiet?"

Josh turned to look out at the quiet road in front of his house and Ross couldn't help wondering if he was avoiding his gaze. "I don't know. Maybe she's blocked out what happened. Lyndsey said that can happen to people when they've been through a traumatic event or something."

What the hell did a sixteen-year-old girl know about dis-association? Ross frowned. "Maybe that's what happened. I don't know. But even if that's the case, I would still like to hear her say so. At this point, I'd like to hear anything—that she can't remember what happened or she's not sure or aliens abducted her and sucked out her memory with their proton beams. Anything at all. I wish she could see that her silence is as good as a confession."

"She didn't do it, though," Josh muttered. "You and I both *know* she didn't. I hate thinking of her in jail."

His voice broke a little on the last word but he quickly cleared his throat, embarrassed, and straightened from the pillar.

Ross rested an awkward hand on Josh's shoulder, wishing he was better at this whole parenting thing. "Your loyalty means the world to her, I know."

To his dismay, instead of taking his words as praise, as Ross intended, Josh seemed even more upset by them. He looked as if Ross had shoved a fist in his solar plexus.

"I'm going to bed," he said after a moment, his voice strangled and tight. "I'll see you later."

"'Night," Ross said and watched with concern as Josh went back inside the house.

These sessions with Julie were a good idea, he decided. He just hoped she could get to the bottom of the kid's odd behavior.

Chapter Eight

"I appreciate you coming out here, son. I know you're busy and I hope it didn't mess up your schedule too much."

As Ross shook his uncle William's hand in the foyer of the Double Crown, he thought how much he respected him. His mother's brother was as unlike Cindy as he imagined two people who came from the same womb could possibly be.

William had always struck him as decent and honorable. Though Ross hadn't known him well growing up because William and his wife and five sons lived in Los Angeles and their respective spheres rarely intersected, his uncle had invariably been kind to him and his brothers and sister when they did.

His wife Molly had died a year ago, and William had temporarily moved from California to Texas and the family ranch just a few months earlier after a string of mysterious incidents threatened the family's security.

Ross thought of the word he had used the night of the

dinner with Julie that had upset Josh so much—*loyalty*. William typified family loyalty. His uncle invariably thought first about the Fortunes and what was in the family's best interest, and Ross had to respect him all the more for it.

"Not a problem," he said now. "I'm staying in Red Rock with Josh anyway so it wasn't any trouble to come out here to the Double Crown."

Before William could answer him, Lily—William and Cindy's cousin by marriage—walked down the stairs.

At sixty-three, she was still exotically lovely from her Apache and Spanish heritage, with high cheekbones, tilt-tipped eyes framed by thick lashes and a wide, sultry mouth.

She was also one of his favorite Fortunes. He would have loved having a mother as warm and caring and maternal as Lily Fortune.

"Ross, my dear. You don't come to the Double Crown enough," she said, gripping his hands and squeezing them tightly.

"Sorry about that. I've been pretty busy lately."

"You've got your hands full right now, don't you? How is Frannie?"

He frowned. He had seen Frannie that morning at the jail— just another frustrating visit. How had he never guessed that such obstinance lurked inside his delicate sister? He had asked, begged and finally pleaded with her to tell him what had happened the night of Lloyd's death, but she remained stubbornly silent.

"I can't talk about it."

That was her only response, every single time he pushed her. Finally she had told him she would tell the guards she wouldn't take any more visits from him if he didn't stop haranguing her about it.

"She doesn't belong in prison. That's for damn sure."

He heard his own language and winced. "Sorry, Lily. For darn sure, I meant."

She rolled her eyes. "If a little colorful language ever sent me into a swoon, I wouldn't be much good on a working ranch, would I?"

Ross grinned. "I suppose not."

"For what it's worth, I completely agree with you. I can't believe that pip-squeak Bruce Gibson was able to get his way and have her held without bail. It's an outrage, that's what it is."

"I couldn't agree more," William put in. "Any word on appealing the judge's decision on bail?"

"The lawyers are working on it." Like everything else, they were in wait-and-see mode.

"Whatever you need, Ross," William said, his expression solemn and sincere. "The family is behind you a hundred percent on this. We can hire different attorneys to argue for a change of venue if that would help."

"I don't know what's going to help at this point. I just need to figure out who really killed Lloyd so I can get her out of there."

"Whatever you need," William repeated. "Just say the word and we'll do anything it takes to help you."

"Thanks, Uncle William. I appreciate that."

He did, though it wasn't an easy thing for him to admit. As much as he respected his Fortune relatives, they had all come to his immediate family's rescue far more often than he could ever find comfortable. Cindy would have sucked the Fortune financial well dry if she could have found a way.

"Come on back to the kitchen, why don't you?" Lily said after a moment. "Rosita made cinnamon rolls this morning and I'm sure there are a few left."

His stomach rumbled, reminding him that breakfast had been coffee and a slice of burnt toast made from one of the last pieces of bread at the house. They were just about out of food. If he didn't want his nephew to starve, he was going to have to schedule a trip to the grocery store soon, as much as he heartily disliked the task.

He couldn't help comparing the big, warm kitchen at the Double Crown with Frannie's elegant, spare kitchen. *This* was the kitchen of his childhood dreams, something he didn't think was a coincidence. On his few trips to the Double Crown as a kid, this place had seemed like heaven on earth, from the horses to the swimming hole to the big rope swing in the barn that sent anyone brave enough for it sailing through the air into soft, clean-smelling hay.

Given a choice, he would much rather slide up to this table, with its scarred top and acres of mismatched chairs, than Frannie's perfect designer set.

Rosita, Lily's longtime friend and housekeeper, bustled around in the kitchen in an old-fashioned ruffled apron. She beamed when she saw Ross and ordered him to sit.

"You are too skinny. You need to come eat in my kitchen more often."

He raised an eyebrow. Only someone as comfortably round as Rosita could ever call him skinny. "If those cinnamon rolls taste as good as they smell, I might just have to kidnap you and take you back to Frannie's mausoleum to cook for Josh and me. We're getting a little tired of ordering pizza."

"You know you and Josh are welcome here anytime," Lily said.

"I wasn't hinting for an invitation," Ross said, embarrassed that his words might have been construed that way.

Lily smiled and squeezed his arm. It took him a moment to realize why the gesture seemed familiar. Julie had the same kind of mannerisms, that almost unconscious way of reinforcing her words with a physical touch.

He had come to crave those casual little brushes of her hands on him, though he would rather be hog-tied and left in a bull paddock than admit it.

They spoke of family news for a few moments while he savored divine mouthfuls of the gooey, yeasty cinnamon rolls. William caught him up on the upcoming wedding of his son Darr to Bethany Burdett, a receptionist at the Fortune Foundation, then Lily shared news about her family.

Ross had never quite figured out his place on the Fortune family tree. Sure, he shared the surname since Cindy had never bothered to change her name through any of her three marriages and had made sure each of her children carried it, as well. But he never quite felt a part of the family.

Cindy had been estranged from her siblings for years. Until Frannie's marriage to Lloyd eighteen years ago gave her more of an excuse, Cindy only popped into Red Rock once in a while, usually to hit somebody in her family up for money.

How many times had his uncle William and aunt Molly bailed Cindy out of some scrape or another? Even Lily and her late husband Ryan had taken a turn.

Ross felt keenly obligated to them all for it—which was exactly why he was here listening to family gossip he didn't really care about and enjoying Rosita's exquisite cinnamon rolls.

"I guess you know the reason we asked you here," William finally said when there was a lull in the conversation. "We're just looking for an update on your investigation."

"Which one?" Ross muttered ruefully, taking a sip of coffee. Right now he felt as if he were spinning three or four dozen plates and was quite sure each one was ready to crash to the ground.

"Finding out the truth behind whoever killed Lloyd has to be your priority right now, for Frannie and Josh's sake. We completely understand that." William paused, his expression serious. "But I hope you understand that my priority right now is keeping the rest of the family safe."

His gaze flickered briefly to Lily just long enough for Ross to wonder if something were going on between the two of them. *William and Lily?* As stunning as he found the idea, it made an odd sort of sense. They each had lost—and mourned—their respective spouses and they were both heavily involved with the Fortune Foundation.

He hadn't heard anything from any other family members about a burgeoning romance between the two of them, but maybe it was still in the early stages.

He had enough genuine mysteries to solve, he reminded himself. He didn't need to concern himself with any hypothetical romance between Lily and William—and it was none of his business anyway.

"Have you discovered anything new about the fires here and at Red or the mysterious notes we've received?" William asked.

In January, a fire nearly destroyed the local restaurant owned by good friends of the Fortunes, the Mendozas. At that same time, William and his brother Patrick each received a mysterious note that said simply "One of the Fortunes is not who you think."

Just a month later, another fire had destroyed a barn at the Double Crown, killing a favorite horse, and Lily had received a note of her own that read "This one wasn't an accident, either."

Ross had been brought in after that, when the family realized all these seemingly random events were connected.

He hadn't been very successful, though, much to his chagrin, both professionally and personally. Then in April, the mystery deepened and became even more sinister when his mother wrecked her car after a visit with Frannie and the Red Rock police discovered that her brakes had been tampered with.

Ross still couldn't completely convince himself Cindy hadn't done it herself for attention. That was a pretty pitiful suspicion for a son to have about his own mother, but he had learned during his forty years on the planet not to put much past her. Still, he was investigating the brake-tampering incident as part of the pattern.

"I'll be honest with you, Uncle William," he said now. "I'm hitting a wall. The private lab I sent the letters to was unable to find any legible fingerprints on either the notepaper itself or the envelopes used, and they were both very generic items that could have been purchased anywhere. Nothing distinctive at all that might help us identify who purchased them and sent them. The lab was able to collect a small amount of DNA from whoever licked the envelopes, but it's not in any of the databanks we can access."

"Which means what, exactly?" Lily asked.

He gave them both an apologetic look. "Until we have a suspect to compare the sample to, DNA doesn't do us much good."

"Where do you suggest we go from here?" William asked, his expression troubled. He slanted a look at Lily and the obvious worry in his eyes made Ross wonder again at their relationship.

"I've still got some leads I'm following on Cindy's brakes and the accelerant used in both fires. But I'll be honest, right now my focus has to be on Frannie."

"That's just as it should be," Lily assured him, her features sympathetic. "I worry so for her. She's such a quiet soul, one who certainly doesn't belong in jail. I hate that she has to go through this."

"What about Josh?" William asked. "In a way, he's lost both a mother and a father, hasn't he?"

"Only temporarily, until I can clear Frannie and get her home where she belongs." He spoke the words in a vow.

Lily touched his arm again, her hands cool and soft. "You're such a good brother, Ross. You always have been. I don't know what would have happened to Frannie or your brothers if not for you."

William made a face. "It was an outrage what you children had to endure. The rest of us should never have allowed it. It's one of my greatest regrets in life that we didn't realize just how bad things were and didn't sue for custody of all of you."

How different his life might have turned out, if that had happened. He might have grown up in California with William and Molly and their sons or here on the ranch with Ryan and his first wife. He might have had breakfast every morning in this big, comfortable kitchen, instead of in whatever dingy apartment Cindy found for them.

"I wish I could say my sister ever outgrew her irresponsibility," William went on, "but she's as flighty and self-destructive at seventy as she was when she was a girl. I'm only sorry she dragged the four of you with her."

The last thing Ross wanted to talk about right now was his mother and the chaos of his childhood and all the might-havebeens that seemed more painful in retrospect. He quickly changed the subject.

"I'll admit, I'm worried about how this is all affecting Josh. He went back to school last week but he won't talk about how things are going. I know how kids can talk and I'm sure a scandal like this is the hot topic at Red Rock High School."

As he hoped, the diversionary tactic did the trick. Lily's eyes grew soft with concern, as they did whenever she heard about a child or youth in need.

"Have you thought about grief counseling for him?" she asked. "Perhaps someone at the Foundation might be able to see him. Julie Osterman, for instance, specializes in helping teens who have suffered loss."

Okay, maybe changing the subject hadn't been the greatest idea. He didn't want to talk about Julie any more than he wanted to discuss Cindy.

He certainly hadn't been able to stop thinking about her since their dinner and the heated kiss they had shared nearly a week before. He had tried everything to get the blasted woman out of his system. He had worked like a maniac tracking down leads in Frannie's case, had taken Josh out fishing three more times, had swum so many laps in his sister's pool he thought he might just grow fins.

But he still dreamed of Julie every night and thoughts of her had a devious way of slithering into his mind at the most inconvenient time. Like, oh, just about every other minute.

"He's actually seeing Julie," Ross admitted. "He's been to a few sessions now. I can't say if they're helping yet."

"Julie is wonderful," Lily exclaimed. "Don't you just love her?"

Ross nearly choked on his coffee. "Um, she seems nice

enough." Somehow he managed not to choke on the under-statement, as well. "Josh likes her and that's the important thing."

"Julie is the perfect one to help him," Lily said. "She understands what it is to lose someone she loved."

"Yeah," Ross said, his voice gruff. "She told me about her husband."

Lily blinked a little at that. "Did she?"

Ross fiddled with his cup. "Yeah."

"What happened?" William asked. "I had no idea she was even married."

Lily touched his hand. "I'll tell you later," she said, then turned back to Ross. "I can't tell you how pleased and relieved I am that Josh is talking to someone. I've been so worried for him, especially since the last words between Josh and Lloyd were so harsh."

Ross frowned. "Harsh? Why do you say that?"

Lily shifted in her chair, looking as if she wished she hadn't said anything. "They were fighting, maybe a half hour before Lloyd was found dead. I'm sorry. I assumed you knew."

Fighting? Josh and Lloyd? This was the first he had heard anything about Josh even seeing his father the night of Lloyd's death. His nephew had never said a word about it.

Why hadn't he? Ross wondered.

"Did you hear them?" he asked.

"It wasn't my intention to eavesdrop. You have to under-stand that. But I left the dance for a moment and returned to the art booths, hoping to catch one of the vendors who was selling a particularly lovely plein air painting I had my eye on. I had talked myself out of it then decided at the last moment that it would be stunning in one of the guest bedrooms here. It *was* perfect, by the way. Would you like to see it?"

Lily was stalling, which wasn't at all like her.

"What did you hear?" he asked.

She sighed. "I was taking the painting to my car when I heard raised voices. I would have walked past, but then I recognized Josh's voice. They were some distance away, behind the exhibits, and I'm sure they didn't see me. I'm not sure they would have noticed anyway. They both sounded so furious."

His gut clenched. Why hadn't Josh mentioned any fight with his father? In the nearly two weeks since the murder, his nephew hadn't said a single word about any altercation. Why the hell not?

"Could you hear what they were saying?" Ross asked, unable to keep the harsh urgency out of his voice.

Lily glanced at William then back at Ross. "Not clearly. I'm sorry, Ross. They were some distance away from me. And though their voices were raised, I couldn't hear everything. Lloyd was mostly yelling at poor Josh about something or other. I heard him call him a careless idiot at one point and he said something else about Josh ruining his life."

"Did you hear Josh's response?" he asked. It suddenly seemed vitally important, for reasons Ross wasn't prepared to analyze.

Again Lily looked at William as if seeking moral support. His uncle looked as concerned as Ross was and he was quite certain this was the first his uncle had heard about an altercation between them, as well.

"He's just a boy," she said. "He didn't mean anything."

"What did he say, Lily?" William picked up her hand and curled his fingers around it. "Tell us."

She sighed. "He said he wouldn't let Lloyd get away with it. Whatever *it* might have been. I couldn't hear that part. And then he said something about how he—Josh—would stop Lloyd, no matter what it took."

The coffee and cinnamon rolls seemed to congeal in Ross's stomach. "Have you told anyone else about this?"

"No." She frowned, suddenly pensive. "But I think Frannie heard their argument, too. In fact, I'm almost certain of it. I saw her just a few moments later and she looked white and didn't even say hello, which was not at all like her."

What else had his family not bothered to tell him? His first instinct was to drive to the high school, yank Josh out of his chemistry final and rip into him for keeping these kinds of secrets.

What had Josh and his father been fighting about? And more importantly, why the hell hadn't Josh told him?

"I'm sorry, Ross. I can see you're upset. I would have told you earlier but I just assumed Josh or Frannie must have mentioned it to you."

"No," he said grimly. "Both of them are apparently keeping their mouths shut about any number of things. But I intend to find out what."

He had learned after more than a decade on the police force and two more years as a private investigator that sometimes he just needed to give his subconscious time and space to chew on things, to sort through all the pieces of a case and help him put them back together in the right order.

Sometimes mundane tasks helped the process, so Ross decided to stop at the grocery store on the way back from the Double Crown.

The wheels were spinning a hundred miles an hour as he pushed the cart through the cereal aisle, trying to remember which were Josh's favorites.

He disliked grocery shopping. Always had. He had a service in San Antonio that delivered the same things to him every week. Milk, eggs, cheese, a variety of frozen dinners. He still had to make the occasional trip to the store but most of the basics were covered by the delivery service.

Yeah, it made him feel like a pathetic old bachelor once in a while, but he figured it was all about time management. Why waste time with a task he disliked when he could pay someone else to take care of it?

He knew why shopping bothered him. He didn't need counseling to figure it out. It was a silly reaction, he knew, but somehow grocery shopping reminded him far too much of those frequent times when Cindy would take off when they were kids—of being nine years old again, pushing five-year-old Frannie in a shopping cart and nagging his six- and seven-year-old brothers to stay with them while he roamed through the aisle trying to figure out what they could afford from the emergency stash he always tried to stockpile with money he stole out of his mother's purse for just these moments.

He pushed back the image as he mechanically moved through the store, trying to remember what kind of food he liked when he was eighteen.

He passed the pharmacy at the front of the store and suddenly saw Jillian Fredericks standing at the counter.

Damn. He was in no mood for a confrontation with the woman right here in the middle of the Piggly Wiggly, for her sake or his own. She had been through enough and he didn't want to dredge up any more pain for her.

Sidestepping to a different aisle was simply the humane,

decent thing to do, he told himself, though slinking through the store made him feel even more like that nine year old of his memory.

He was so intent on avoiding Jillian that he didn't notice anybody else in the aisle until someone called his name.

"Ross. Hello! How are you?"

He lifted his gaze from the detergent bottles and found Julie Osterman standing just across the aisle from him.

To his eternal chagrin, his heart did a crazy little tap dance at the sight of her.

She glanced at the few items in his cart. "Please tell me you and Josh are eating something besides cold cereal and potato chips."

He felt his face heat. "We had steak the other night with you. And we've gone to Red a few times. Tonight we're ordering pizza."

She didn't roll her eyes but he could tell she wanted to. Instead, she gave a rueful smile. "I won't nag."

He didn't want to think about the way her concern for their diet sent a traitorous warmth uncurling through him. "But you'd like to."

She opened her mouth to answer, but sighed instead. "Just remember, he's right in the middle of finals. A balanced meal here or there won't hurt."

"I'll have Mel down at the pizza parlor throw on extra vegetables, how about that?"

"Sounds perfect." She smiled, her lovely blue eyes bright and amused, and he suddenly couldn't think about anything but the heat and wonder of that blasted kiss. "You're not working today?" he asked.

"It's my afternoon off. Usually I try to catch up on my reports at home where it's quiet but I've been putting off grocery shopping and I decided to check that task off my list this afternoon."

"It's a pain in the neck, isn't it?"

She looked surprised. "I kind of like shopping. All those possibilities in front of me. I can walk out of the store with the makings of a gourmet supper or I can just run in for a glazed doughnut that's lousy for me but tastes divine. It all depends on my mood."

"Must be a girl thing."

She laughed and he realized how much brighter the world suddenly seemed than when he walked into the store. It was an uncomfortable discovery, that she could affect his entire mood just with her presence.

"How's Josh doing today?"

"That seems to be the question of the day. I wish I could tell people some answer other than 'fine.' He doesn't talk much to me about it."

He hadn't pushed the boy, but after his conversation with Lily, he was beginning to think that had been a mistake.

"That's completely normal, Ross," she answered. "Most seventeen-year-old boys would much prefer going outside and shooting hoops to sitting around discussing their emotional mood of the moment."

"I think it's probably fair to say most forty-year-old men aren't much different."

She laughed softly and he was suddenly consumed with the desire to taste that delectable mouth again, right there beside the fabric softeners. He even leaned forward slightly, then caught himself and jerked back.

Josh, he reminded himself. Focus on Josh. The conversation with Lily came back to him. Had Josh told Julie about his fight with his father the night of his death?

"Josh talks to you, though, right? I mean, you've had two sessions with him now."

"Yes," she said, somewhat warily.

"Did he mention anything about talking to his father the night of the Spring Fling?" he asked.

She sighed. "You know I can't tell you anything about my conversations with him, Ross. They're confidential. Right now Josh is still willing to talk to me and I don't want to do anything to jeopardize the trust he has in me. I'm sorry."

Sometimes he really hated when people were decent and honorable.

That didn't mean he always had to play by the same rules. A good investigator could read as much in what a person *didn't* say—in her body language and her facial expressions—as in her words. He had learned that sometimes offering information of his own could elicit the reaction he needed to verify his suspicions.

"I had an interesting conversation with someone today who said she overheard Josh and his father in a bitter argument shortly before Lloyd's death," he said with studied casualness. "I was just going to ask if he had said anything to you about it."

Julie was pretty adept at hiding her reaction to his words—but not quite good enough. He didn't miss how her eyes widened with surprise and the ever-so-slight way her lips parted just for an instant.

So Josh *hadn't* mentioned the fight to Julie in their sessions. *Why not?* he wondered, concerned all over again at what other secrets his nephew might be keeping.

"Do you think that's pertinent to investigating what might have happened that night?" she asked.

He shrugged. "I can't say. I just find it surprising that Josh hasn't bothered to mention it. He never even told me he saw his father at the Spring Fling. Even though he claimed to hate Lloyd, I imagine it's got to be tough on any kid to know the last words he had with his old man were angry ones."

Not that he would know. His own father had left Cindy when Ross was less than a year old. Riley Randolph hadn't exactly been the fatherly type. Big surprise there, that Cindy would pick that kind of husband.

"If you're trying to get me to divulge anything from our therapy sessions," Julie said with a frown, "I'm afraid I can't help you."

Sweetheart, you already have, he thought. While he wouldn't exactly call her transparent, she was far too open a person to keep all her reactions concealed.

"I just wanted to pass on information," he said, which wasn't completely a lie. "Thought it might help you to have a little more background on that night when you're talking to Josh. You could ask him in the next session why they fought."

And why he hasn't bothered to tell anyone, he added silently.

"Thank you, Ross. I appreciate the information, then."

They lapsed into silence and Ross thought he probably ought to be moving his cart along, but he was suddenly loath to leave. He searched for some excuse to prolong their conversation, even as some part of his mind was fully aware of how pathetic it was that he was so conflicted over her.

He told himself every time he was with her that he needed to keep his distance. But then the next time he saw her, he was drawn to her all over again.

He knew he shouldn't find it such a consolation that she didn't seem in a hurry to leave his company, either.

"Josh told me it is his eighteenth birthday this weekend. What are his plans?" she asked.

He seized on the question. "Actually, I'm glad you brought that up. While I have you here, I could use some advice."

"Sure."

"We have to do something to celebrate his birthday. I mean, a kid only turns eighteen once. But I'm wondering if you've got any suggestions about what might be appropriate. Before everything happened, Frannie had talked about throwing a big party for him, but that doesn't seem right now, given the circumstances."

"That's a really good question." Her brow furrowed. "What would make Josh happiest? What might help him forget for a few hours all that's happened in his world?"

"I think he got a kick out of going out to the lake last week. We could do that again." He paused. "And he has that girlfriend, Lyndsey. Maybe I could have a barbecue that night and invite her and a few of his other friends."

"That sounds like a wonderful idea, Ross. See, you're better at this whole parenthood thing than you give yourself credit for."

He wasn't, though. He had sucked at it when he was a kid forced to take care of his younger siblings and he didn't feel any more capable now.

"Will you help me?"

The question came out of nowhere, surprising him as much as it did her.

"Help you how?" she asked, that wariness in her eyes again.

So much for keeping his distance from her. Ross sighed. But now that he had asked her, it made sense. He really *could* use help. It would certainly be easier on his self-control if that help came from someone else, but it was too late to back down now.

"I'm not sure I can handle throwing a teenage party by myself, even a little one," he admitted. "Sure, I can grill steaks and maybe some burgers but other than that, I wouldn't know where to start."

He thought he caught a flash of reluctance in her eyes and he felt foolish for asking. He had already dragged her into their lives too much.

"Never mind," he said. "I'll just get some pop and open a few bags of chips. We should be fine."

She let out a long breath. "I can help you. I don't have any plans Saturday. Why don't you take care of the grill and I'll handle all the other details? The side dishes, the chips, the cake and ice cream."

"Are you sure?"

"No problem." She smiled, with no trace of that hesitation he thought he had seen and he wondered if he had been mistaken. "It will be fun."

Fun. Right.

She was an idiot.

Julie sat in her car in the parking lot of the grocery store for several moments after she had loaded her groceries into the trunk of her car.

She had absolutely no willpower when it came to Ross Fortune. Since that stunning kiss they had shared the week before, she had promised herself she would do her best to return things to a casual friendship.

For the sake of her psyche, she had no other choice. It was painfully obvious he wasn't available for anything else. He had made it quite clear that he only wanted her help with Josh, not for anything else.

She was happy to help with Josh. But she wasn't at all

certain she could continue to do so when she was beginning to entertain all sorts of inappropriate thoughts about the teen's uncle.

She couldn't afford to let herself care for Ross, not when they obviously wanted far different things from life.

A woman came out of the store and pushed her cart to the minivan beside Julie's car. She had a preschool-aged boy hanging off her cart and a curly-haired baby in the cart. The baby was perhaps nine months old, in a pink outfit with bright flowers.

The boy said something to his mother that Julie couldn't hear but the mother laughed and kissed the child on the nose before she picked up the baby to settle her in her car seat.

As she watched them, Julie's heart turned over.

That was what she wanted. She was ready for children of her own, for a family. Seven years had passed since Chris's death and in all the ways that mattered, she had been alone for the last few years of their marriage before that.

She was tired of it. She was ready to move forward with her life. She had even talked to Linda Jamison, the Foundation director, about adopting an older child as a single mother. She had so much love inside her and she wanted somewhere to give it beyond her clients.

Allowing herself to become any more entangled with a man like Ross Fortune would jeopardize all that progress she had made these past seven years toward healing and peace. She sensed it with a certainty she couldn't deny.

Oh, they might have a brief affair that would probably be intense and passionate and wonderful while it lasted.

But Julie knew she would end up more alone than ever. Alone and heartbroken.

The mother beside her finished loading her groceries and

her children and backed out of the parking lot. Julie watched them go with renewed determination.

She would help Ross with Josh's birthday party and that would be the end of it. If he asked for her help with his nephew again, she would politely tell him she was only available in a professional capacity for more counseling sessions.

It would hurt, she knew. She was already coming to care for him and Josh too much. But she didn't see she had any other choice.

She'd already lost too much to risk her heart again.

Chapter Nine

Two days later, she was working on paperwork in her office when Susan Fortune Eldridge poked her head in the doorway.

"Hey," her friend and coworker exclaimed. "I haven't talked to you in ages. It seems like we're always running in different directions. How are things?"

"Good," Julie answered. "Busy, as usual. How about you?"

"Great. Wonderful, really. Listen, Ethan and I are throwing an impromptu dinner party this weekend. We thought maybe you could bring Sean or whatever is the name of that art teacher you're seeing."

Julie couldn't help but laugh. "I would certainly do that, but I'm not sure his fiancée would appreciate it."

Susan's green eyes opened wide and she moved fully into Julie's office and sat in the easy chair her clients usually took. "Fiancée? When did that happen?"

"A few weeks ago, from what I understand. I bumped into

him the other day at the library and he told me about it. He started seeing her not long after we stopped dating, around New Year's."

Susan made a face. "Some friend I am. You broke up with someone five months ago and I'm only just hearing about it? Why didn't I know?"

"We didn't really break up. We just mutually decided that while we enjoyed each other's company, we didn't have that sizzle. We only dated a few times anyway. It was never anything serious."

Unfortunately, their brief relationship had coincided with the holiday party season and Sean had escorted her to several parties around town that Susan and her veterinarian husband Ethan had also attended. Julie could completely understand why she might have been under the impression they were more serious than they were.

"Well, bring whoever you're seeing now," Susan said. "It's obviously been too long since we socialized outside the office, since I apparently have no idea what's going on in your life."

Julie had a quick mental image of the heated kiss with Ross that she couldn't get out of her head. She had a feeling Susan would probably misunderstand if she mentioned that particular encounter.

"When is your party?" she asked.

"Tomorrow night. Around seven."

She winced. "I'm sorry, Susan, but I already have plans tomorrow."

"Oh? Hot date? Tell me all!"

"Nothing to tell, I'm afraid. Um, I told your cousin Ross I would help him throw a small party for Josh's eighteenth birthday."

"I completely forgot Josh's birthday was coming up." She paused, an expression of concern on her petite features. "So tell me. How is Ross doing?"

"Fine, as far as I can tell. Why do you ask? Usually everyone seems to be most concerned with Frannie or Josh."

"I've been worrying about him. I've tried to call a few times to check on him and Josh and always get voice mail. We've been playing phone tag. I was planning on making time this weekend to go to the house to see how things are with them. This can't be an easy situation for Ross."

She frowned. "What can't?"

"The instant parenting thing landing in his lap so abruptly. I've always had the impression he wanted nothing to do with kids and parenting after his lousy childhood. He probably figured he did his share while practically raising his brothers and sister."

Julie suddenly realized how little she knew about Ross's past. She knew he had been a cop in San Antonio but his life before then was a mystery. "Where were his parents?"

"I don't know about his dad. I think he took off when Ross was just a baby. I don't know about him or the other fathers."

"Other…fathers?"

"Frannie's his half sister and he has two half brothers, Cooper and Flint. They all have different fathers, except the middle boys. None of the men stuck around for long, except Frannie's dad, I guess, who might have if he hadn't died first."

"How sad!"

"Yes, well, my aunt Cindy certainly knows how to pick them."

"That's Ross's mother?"

"She's the woman who gave birth to him, anyway," Susan

answered. "Calling her a mother might be a bit of a stretch. She was sister to my father, Leonard, as well as Patrick and William."

Julie frowned. "I'm not sure I've met her."

"Believe me, you would remember if you had. Cindy is a real piece of work, let me tell you. She wears tons of makeup and still dresses like a hootchie-kootchie dancer, which I've heard rumors she was, in between stints as a showgirl in Vegas."

"Wow."

"Right. She's seventy years old and still dresses in tight pants and halter tops."

"Sounds like an interesting character," she said faintly.

"*Interesting* is one word for it. From family gossip, I've heard she ran off to Vegas to be a dancer when she was barely eighteen. She had a long string of lousy relationships and three marriages. During that time, she gave birth to Ross and his siblings but I don't think she had much to do with raising them. She was too busy shaking her booty in one club or another."

Julie tried to imagine Ross growing up under those circumstances and couldn't. No wonder he seemed so hard and cynical if that was the only example of a family he had.

"Ross was the oldest," Susan went on. "Frannie told me once that he was always the one who fixed her hair, packed her lunch and sent her off to school. Cindy was always either entertaining company or too tired from working into the night. He kept that family together, dysfunctional as it was."

Julie thought of her own family, warm and loving and completely supportive of whatever she had ever tried to do. During those dark and terrible times during Chris's illness and then after his suicide, she had moved back home with her parents in Austin and they had enfolded her with loving arms of support and comfort.

Her four brothers might drive her crazy sometimes with their overprotectiveness but she adored them all.

What must Ross's childhood have been like? She tried to picture a younger version of the hard, implacable man she knew trying to fix his little sister's hair and the image just about broke her heart.

"I've always wanted to see him happy," Susan went on. "Settled, you know, with a home and family. I don't know if I'd say he's really happy, but he seems content with his bachelor life. It's terribly sad, really, when you think about it. I wonder what scars he still carries from such an unstable childhood."

Julie knew it was ridiculous to feel this sudden urge to cry. She fought back the tears and hoped Susan didn't notice her reaction.

"I've worried that his temporary guardianship of Josh—again, someone else's child he's suddenly responsible for—must in a sense feel like he's reliving his own childhood," Susan said. "I've been worried about his head and wanted to make sure he's in an okay place about the whole thing."

"I had no idea," Julie said. "Ross never said anything."

Susan gave her a curious look, which quickly turned speculative. "Why would he have told you? I wasn't under the impression you knew Ross well, other than in your capacity as Josh's grief counselor."

Her eyes suddenly widened. "Which begs the question—why, again, are you helping with Josh's party? That seems above and beyond the call of duty, no matter how wonderful a counselor you are."

Julie ordered herself not to blush. "Ross asked for my help. I couldn't say no."

Her friend was quiet for a long moment, then she tilted her head, giving Julie a searching look. "Is there something between you and my cousin?"

Did a heated kiss and a fierce attraction she couldn't seem to shove out of her head count as something? Her face felt hot and she couldn't meet Susan's gaze.

"We've become friends, I guess you could say."

"Only friends?"

"I don't think he's available for anything else right now."

She regretted the words as soon as she said them. As a psychologist, Susan was an expert at analyzing people's words, sifting through layers of nuances and meaning to help her have better clarity into their psyches. Julie realized too late how her words must have sounded—and she heard the echo of the ruefulness in her voice.

"If he were?" Susan asked, studying her closely.

She let out a breath. "Since that's a rhetorical question, I don't really have to answer it, do I?"

Susan was silent for a long time. When she finally spoke, her eyes were soft with concern. "I love Ross, Julie. If I could pick anyone in the world for him, she would be someone exactly like you. Someone nurturing and caring and generous. Someone who could help him heal."

Since Julie was also trained to listen carefully to her clients and parse through their words, she didn't miss how Susan had phrased her comment. "Someone exactly like me, but not me?"

"I love Ross," Susan repeated. "But I love you, too. You've been through so much pain. I ache just thinking about what you've had to survive. You deserve a man whose heart is healthy and strong, someone who is free to love you without reservation."

"And you don't think that's Ross."

Susan's silence was a harsh answer. Julie reminded herself she had known. Hadn't she promised herself she would give him one more night for Josh's birthday party and then try to extricate herself from his life so she could move forward?

Still, she couldn't deny the spasm of pain and regret twisting through her at having her own convictions reinforced.

"Then it's a good thing Ross and I are only friends, isn't it?" she said briskly. "I'm only helping him with a birthday party, Sus. That's all."

"Sure." Susan forced a smile. "Well, I'm sorry you can't come to our dinner party. We'll do it another time, then. Give Josh a big birthday kiss for me, okay? And tell Ross I'll keep trying to reach him."

Unexpectedly, Susan hugged her on the way out the door. She hugged her back, then returned to work, trying her best to shake the discontent pulling at her mood like heavy, intractable weights.

Ross pulled into the circular driveway in front of Frannie's house, fighting off the bleak mood that settled over him as he looked at it. There was no reason such a silly froth of a house should seem so ominous, but he had begun to dread coming back here each night.

Josh wasn't home. The boy's aging sports car wasn't in the driveway and Ross knew damn well he shouldn't have this vague feeling of relief that he didn't have to deal with his nephew right now.

He was going to have to talk to him sometime. A serious, blunt conversation between the two of them was long overdue. Ross rubbed his temples as the implication of all he had learned over the last two days centered there in a pounding headache that slithered down his spine to his tight shoulders until it became a cold, greasy ball in his gut.

He still didn't want to believe any of it, but it was becoming increasingly difficult to keep an open mind.

After his talk with Lily and William at the Double Crown, he had spent two days tracking down leads, trying to find anyone else who might have heard Josh fighting with his father and who might be able to shed more light on the content of their conversation. He wanted to be prepared with as much information as possible before he faced his nephew with what he had learned.

He finally found a potter whose stall had been not far from the scene of the argument. Reynaldo Velasquez had indeed heard the fight. He had recounted it much as Lily had—that he couldn't hear many of the words but he had heard raised voices, had heard Lloyd yelling at his son and then had heard Josh say he would stop him, no matter what it took.

And, more chilling than that confirmation, Reynaldo had added that he had been surprised to hear such harsh words coming from Josh. He'd seemed like a nice kid, the artist said, when he had come to his booth to pick up the large vase his mother had purchased earlier in the evening.

Ross closed his eyes, his hands tight on the steering wheel. Even now, remembering the conversation, his stomach felt slick with nausea. As far as he could tell, Josh had been the last one in possession of the vase.

Josh. Not Frannie.

Josh had fought with his father in front of witnesses. Josh had a rocky relationship with his father. Josh was a hot-headed teenager.

And most damning of all was Josh's behavior since his

father's death. The furtive conversations, the obfuscations. Ross had sensed he was hiding something. He supposed it made him a pretty damn lousy investigator that he hadn't once suspected his nephew was capable of killing his own father.

Despite the witnesses and Josh's own dishonesty by omission in not saying anything about the fight with Lloyd, Ross still couldn't make himself believe it, any more than he had been able to contemplate the ridiculous notion that Frannie might have killed Lloyd.

Josh was a good kid. Yeah, he had a temper and his relationship with Lloyd was tense and strained and had been for some time now. But Ross couldn't accept that Josh might be able to commit patricide. And he absolutely couldn't see the boy he knew standing by and saying nothing while his own mother took the fall for it.

Ross would have to talk to him about what he had learned, no matter how difficult the conversation. He would have to walk a fine line between seeking the vital information he needed to put these pieces of the puzzle together without sounding accusatory. It would take every ounce of his investigative skills.

He didn't want to ruin Josh's birthday, but he had no choice. Josh would legally be an adult in just a few hours. Perhaps it was past time Ross started treating him like one.

With a sigh, he let himself into the house. The empty foyer echoed with every sound he made, from the clink of his keys on the polished white table to the scrape of his boots on the tile floor.

He hated it here. He found the entire place depressing. He had never liked it, even when Frannie was here, but without her, the house seemed lifeless and cold.

He had a sudden, irrational, very Cindy-like desire to walk

away from everything here, to escape back to his apartment in San Antonio where he had no responsibilities except to his agency clients. Where he was free to come and go at will, without this nagging worry for those he loved.

Ashamed of himself for indulging the impulse to flee, even for a moment, he walked through the house to the kitchen and flipped on the light switch.

The first thing he saw was a note from Josh on the memo board above the small kitchen desk that Frannie had always kept meticulously organized. It was written in Josh's careless scrawl on the back of a takeout menu for the pizza parlor.

Helping a friend. Don't wait up.

Ross frowned. Helping which friend do what, where? The kid was a few hours away from eighteen and now thought he could come and go as he pleased without any more explanation than one terse, say-nothing note?

Fighting down that instinctive relief again that he could put off the coming interrogation for a while longer, he pulled out his cell phone and hit Josh's number. The phone rang four times then went to voice mail.

Ross sighed. "Call me," he said after the beep, not unaware of the terseness of his own message.

He thought about dinner, but he didn't have much of an appetite anyway, he decided. A better expenditure of time would be to enter the field notes from his interview with Reynaldo into his case file.

He headed down the hall to the guest room he had taken over for his use since coming to stay at the house. Compared to the rest of the house, this room was simply decorated, with a double pine bed, dresser and a comfortable desk. He figured Lloyd hadn't bothered to come into it enough to insist on more of his atrocious taste.

Ross set his laptop case on the bed and pulled out the digital recorder and the small notebook he used on field interviews.

An hour later, he finished logging in his work for the day. Since the notebook was nearly full, he opened the desk drawer to find a new one and his gut suddenly clenched.

Something wasn't right.

He had a strict system of organization with his case files. He kept the field notebooks he used in numbered order, meticulously dated and filed so he could easily double-check information on any case when needed. No matter what else was going on, he always took the time to refile them in order.

The notebook on top of the stack was *not* the most recent. He frowned and flipped through the half-dozen books he had filled with various casework in the days since coming to stay with Josh.

None of them was in order, the way he was absolutely certain he had left them just that morning.

He stared at the stack as that greasy ball in his gut seemed to take a few more rotations. He might be haphazard and casual about some things—his clothing came to mind and, yeah, he needed a haircut—but not about work. Never about his cases and the interviews.

He couldn't afford to be careless as a private investigator. He had to be able to find information quickly and reliably. And while the computer was a great backup for storing data, he still depended on his own handwritten field notes.

Someone had rifled through his notes. He should have locked them up, but the thought had never even occurred to him.

His mind sorted through other possibilities. He wanted to think maybe he had just been sloppy the last time he was in here. That would be a much more palatable option than what he was beginning to suspect, but he couldn't lie to himself.

He knew without a doubt that he hadn't left his notebooks like this. Which meant someone else had rifled through them.

He only had one suspect and it was the very one he didn't want to believe capable of it. Josh. Who else could it have been? The boy had access to the notebooks and plenty of opportunity when Ross wasn't here. He never bothered to lock the desk drawer. That heedlessness on his part had obviously been a mistake, but Ross had never considered it, had never believed for a moment it might even be necessary.

But motive. Why would Josh want to know what Ross was digging into, unless he had reason to want that information to stay buried?

It was another good question. He now had several for his nephew—if only he could find the kid.

By 8:00 p.m., he still hadn't reached Josh.

Ross paced the living room of Frannie's house, not sure whether to be angry or worried about his nephew, especially when all his calls started going directly to voice mail.

He had been through this waiting game enough with his brothers. He couldn't count the number of nights he had sat up stewing while he waited for either Flint or Cooper to come home, hours later than they were supposed to. Of course, this was a little different situation, since he had never been preparing to question his brothers about a murder.

When his cell phone rang at eight-thirty, he lunged for it.

"Yeah?" he growled.

A slight pause met him then he heard Julie Osterman's voice. "Ross? Is that you?"

His hopes that he might be able to clear everything up quickly with Josh and get the kid home faded.

"Oh. Hi."

A slight pause met his response. "That's a bit of a disheartening reaction," Julie said, her voice suddenly tight. "I just needed to ask a question about tomorrow but I can call back later. Or not."

He cursed under his breath. "Sorry. It's not you, I swear. I'm always glad to talk to you." He probably shouldn't have said that, even though it wasn't a lie. "I was just hoping you were Josh."

She picked up his concern right away. "Josh? Is something wrong? What's going on? Where is he?"

"No idea. He's not answering his cell. He left a note saying he was helping a friend and that I wasn't to wait up."

"But of course you will."

"Oh, undoubtedly," he said grimly. "I have a few words to say to my nephew."

"When did you see him last?"

"This morning at breakfast. Everything seemed okay. Nothing out of the ordinary. He left for school to take his last final. We talked about the kids he had invited tomorrow and what movie they planned to watch after dinner. Nothing unusual."

"He didn't say anything about going anywhere after school?"

"Not a word."

But then Ross had kept secrets of his own. He hadn't mentioned anything about the direction he was taking in the investigation because he had wanted to be more certain of his information before confronting Josh about the fight with his father. "He took a call, said something about being on his way, then took off for school."

"Are you sure he went to school?"

"No. But the school's long closed. Unless I drag the principal in from home to go through the attendance records, I'm out of luck."

"What about his other friends? Did you try Lyndsey's cell phone?"

"I don't have her number. I called her home, though, and got no answer."

"What about Ricky or one of his extended cousins?"

"Good idea. I was planning to give him a little longer before I hit the phones."

He didn't tell Julie he would have done that before, but he had still been holding out the vague hope that Josh would walk through the door on his own.

She was quiet for a long moment. "You know, Ross, it's a natural human reaction when life becomes too stressful to seek escape. Perhaps he just needed a little time away from things here in Red Rock."

He hated to ask, in light of her own firsthand experience with suicide, but he had to know her professional opinion. "You're right. Things have been tough for him lately. You don't think he would do anything rash, do you?"

She was silent for a moment and he knew she guessed what he meant. "I couldn't say definitely, but in our two sessions, I didn't get any vibe like that from him, Ross. He wouldn't have any reason to, would he?"

A guilty conscience, maybe? Ross thought of those disordered notebooks and what he had learned the last two days. He hoped Josh didn't feel hopeless or cornered enough to do something drastic.

"I'm going to go look for him," he said suddenly. "I can't just sit here."

Chapter Ten

Julie heard the desperate determination in Ross's voice and she ached for him, especially in light of her conversation with his cousin earlier in the day. He was a man who took his responsibilities seriously and right now he had far too many.

"I'll come with you," she said. "I can be there in fifteen minutes."

"You don't have to do that," he exclaimed, not bothering to hide his surprise that she would make the offer.

"I know I don't. But a second pair of eyes wouldn't hurt, don't you agree? And I have a few advantages."

"What are those?"

"From my clients at the Foundation, I happen to know the location of many of the local teen hangouts. I also have connections among the different teen groups, from the jocks to the druggies to the cowboys to the hackers. I can help you, Ross, if you let me."

She kept her fingers crossed even as she went to her closet and pulled out a jacket and sturdy walking shoes.

Silence met her assurances as he hesitated and she was certain he would refuse her offer of help. Ross was a man who liked to do things on his own, she was learning. He hated depending on anyone else for anything, even for assistance he might desperately need.

She was bracing to tell him she would go on her own looking for Josh when he surprised her.

"All right," he answered. "I probably *could* use your help, especially given your connections to the local teen scene. But stay at your place and I'll come pick you up."

Julie quickly changed out of her lounge-around-the-house sweats into jeans and a tailored blue shirt and sweater and pulled her hair into a ponytail.

While she waited, she went to work gathering a few provisions and compiling lists of any possible friends she might have ever heard Josh mention and several potential places they could look.

When Ross pulled into her driveway exactly sixteen minutes later, she was ready. She opened the door to her house before he could walk up the steps.

He drove a white SUV hybrid that she imagined was perfect for a private investigator—bland enough to be inconspicuous but sturdy enough to be taken seriously.

She opened the door to the back seat and set the large wicker basket inside before she opened the front passenger door and climbed inside.

In the pale glow from the dome light, she could see baffled consternation on his rugged features. "What's all this?" he asked, gesturing to the basket.

She shrugged, feeling slightly foolish. "A few supplies. A

Thermos of coffee, some soda, a few snacks, sandwiches. I didn't know what might come in handy so I packed a little of everything."

He glanced at the overflowing basket in the back seat and then back at her as if he didn't quite know what to make of her. "We're not heading out on a cross-country trek here. We're only driving around town looking for one kid."

"It doesn't hurt to be prepared, does it? You never know what might come in handy." She swiveled in the front seat and reached back to pull a flowered tin off the top of the basket. "Here, have one of my caramel cashew bars. I made them for Josh's birthday tomorrow but I thought maybe we could use them for bribes or something."

"For bribes."

She shrugged. "You know, to get somebody to talk who doesn't want to."

He opened his mouth for a second, his eyes astonished, then closed it with a snap. "That good, are they?" he finally said.

She managed a smile, despite her worry for Josh. "See for yourself."

After a moment's hesitation, he picked one up and bit into it. As he chewed it slowly and then swallowed, his eyes glazed with sheer ecstasy.

"Okay. You win," he said after a few more bites. "Right now, I would tell you anything you want to know."

She laughed, though a hundred questions tumbled together in her mind she would have asked him if circumstances between them had been different.

She held out the tin. "I've got a dozen more in here. You're welcome to eat them all if you want."

He gave her a half smile as he put the SUV into gear before

backing out of her driveway. "Wrong thing to say to an ex-cop," he said. "We're like locusts. If there's food available, we eat it."

She had a sudden wild urge to make a hundred different home-baked treats for him. Dutch apple pie, jam thumbprint cookies, snickerdoodles.

It was a silly reaction but she couldn't help remembering all the bleak details Susan had told her about Ross's childhood. His mother didn't sound like the sort to cook up a batch of warm, gooey chocolate chip cookies for her kids after school and Julie wanted suddenly to make up for all those things Ross never had.

She sighed and pushed the impulse away. Right now they needed to concentrate on Josh, she reminded herself.

"Where to first?" she asked.

"Nobody answered at his girlfriend Lyndsey's house but I figured that's a logical place to start."

The small tract house was in a neighborhood with dozens more that looked just like it. The siding might be a little different color and a few details varied from house to house, but Julie would be hard-pressed to tell them all apart, if not for the house numbers.

No lights were on inside and only a low-wattage porch light glowed on the exterior.

"Doesn't look like anybody's home," he said.

"Her mom works nights," Julie said. "Josh told me that once in passing. I think she's a nurse or something."

"Well, it doesn't hurt to double-check since we're here."

Julie opted to stay in the SUV while Ross walked to the front door and rang the bell. Even with her vehicle window rolled up, she could hear a dog's deep-throated barks from somewhere in the backyard.

The neighborhood shouldn't have seemed ominous. It had

obviously seen better days and some of the houses had peeling paint, with a few junk cars up on cinderblocks in the driveways, but it was equally obvious that families lived here. She spotted multiple bikes, trampolines, play sets.

Still, she was immensely grateful for Ross's solid presence. She wouldn't want to be here by herself.

She watched him ring the doorbell once more, then to her surprise, he reached down and tried to jiggle the doorknob, without success.

"Would you have gone in if the door hadn't been locked?" she asked when he returned to the SUV a moment later.

He shrugged and she didn't miss the gleam of his smile in the darkness. "Don't know," he admitted. "I'm always glad when the opportunity doesn't present itself to find out exactly how far I'm willing to push the law I've always tried to uphold. Any ideas where to try next?"

"Actually, yes. I made a list."

"Why doesn't that surprise me?" Ross asked, a rueful tone to his voice. "Something tells me I'm going to need another caramel cashew bar."

By midnight, they had run out of friends that either of them had ever heard Josh mention. They had hit all the usual hangouts—the quarry, the pizza place, the lover's lane that curved through a forested area south of town. They had even checked beneath the bleachers on the football field.

On a Friday night the week before graduation, they had interrupted a group of half-stoned skinny-dipping seniors, found a half-dozen cars with steamed up windows and nearly found themselves in the middle of a verbal altercation that looked to have been shaping up into one heck of a fistfight.

All the way around, it seemed an exciting night for Red Rock. But Josh was nowhere to be found.

In the parking lot of the high school—their last stop—Julie leaned against the hood of his SUV while Ross stood next to her and dialed the number to the police station.

It was a last resort, a call he didn't want to make, but he thought there might be a slim chance Josh might have tried to contact his mother.

To his surprise—and consternation—he was patched right through to the police chief and he had an instant's sinking fear that Josh might be in custody.

"Hey, Jimmy. It's Ross Fortune."

"Oh. Ross. Hello. This is a surprise. A little late for social calls, isn't it?"

"Yeah, it's late. Oddly enough, you're still there. I wouldn't have thought the Red Rock police chief would pull the graveyard shift. Is something up?"

Jimmy hesitated just long enough for Ross to figure out his guess was correct. He drew a deep breath. *Damn it, Josh. What have you done?*

"Just another wild Friday night in Red Rock. You know how it is. The high schoolers are done with finals so they're all a little nuts. We're busting 'em like crazy on underage drinking and some minor drug possessions."

Ross thought about narcing out the skinny dippers at the quarry, then figured he'd let Jimmy's officers find the party on their own.

"We're a little busy tonight," the police chief said after a moment. "What can I do for you?"

He picked his words delicately. "I'm looking for my sister's kid, Josh. Any chance he stopped in to visit her tonight?"

The police chief was silent for a long moment that seemed to last forever and Ross held his breath, aware of Julie watching the one-sided conversation carefully.

"Not today," Jimmy finally said. "Think he came by earlier in the week. Just a minute. I can call the visitor log up on my computer to double-check for you."

Ross could hear keys clicking and then a moment later, the police chief came back on. "Nope. He was here on Tuesday but hasn't been back. Why do you ask?"

Ross debated telling him the kid had taken off but decided that information could wait. Jimmy was too damn smart and just might look at the puzzle pieces and come up with the same picture Ross was beginning to find.

"Oh, Frannie just asked for some warm socks and I wondered if Josh had had a chance to take them to her. No big deal. I'll stop by with them tomorrow."

"You sure that's all it is?"

They were both circling around each other like a couple of mangy old junkyard dogs after the same bone. "Positive. That's it. You know women and their cold feet."

"Don't I ever!" He gave a jovial laugh that sounded false to Ross's ears, but he wondered if he was imagining things. "Christy Lee just about freezes me out every night. Her feet can be like two little popsicles on the end of her legs."

"Well, thanks for the information. Guess I'll see you tomorrow when I drop off the socks."

"You be sure to do that."

After Ross hung up, he gazed out at the night, replaying the conversation in his head. Something didn't fit with his usual interactions with the police chief.

"Josh hasn't been at the police station?"

"Not that the chief was willing to tell me, anyway."

"Maybe he didn't know."

"There's not much happens at the Red Rock police station that Jimmy doesn't keep an eye on."

It made no sense for the chief to be at the station this late at night unless something big was going down. But short of busting into the police station, Ross had no way of knowing if Josh was there confessing to a murder.

And he could only hope that Josh would have the presence of mind to make a lousy phone call first before he did anything so rash.

"I think we need to check back at the house and see if he came home," Ross said. "I left a big note for him to call me on my cell but maybe he didn't see it."

She looked doubtful and he didn't add that the police station was on the way and that maybe they would just casually take a little drive through the parking lot, looking for a beat-up yellow RX-7.

He didn't see Josh's car in the parking lot of the police station, though. Nor was it in the driveway of Frannie's house.

He must have cursed aloud because Julie reached a comforting hand to touch his forearm. "I'm sure he's fine, Ross. He'll probably turn up any minute, full of apologies and explanations."

"I hope so," he muttered. He led the way inside the house and went immediately to the answering machine. It was blinking to indicate a new message and he stabbed the button.

To his vast relief, Josh's tenor filled the kitchen.

"Hey, Uncle Ross. Sorry, I must have left my phone somewhere in the…somewhere. It was almost out of juice anyway. Anyway, I can't find it right now so I'm calling from a pay phone. Since I couldn't remember your cell number, I'm leaving a message here and hoping you get it.

Don't worry about me. I've got a few things I need to take care of. I don't know when I'll be back but I'm fine, I promise. Everything's fine. Don't worry about me! Just take care of my mom and I'll be back as soon as I can. Thanks, Ross. Sorry about the fishing trip in the morning. Tell Ms. O to forget about the dinner, too. I'll make it up to you both, I promise."

Ross looked at the time stamp on the message and growled a harsh curse. "We only missed his call by half an hour."

"He said he was calling from a pay phone," Julie said. "Did the number show up on the caller ID? I don't know how these things are done but maybe you could trace it and at least narrow down where he was a half hour ago."

"Great idea." He scrolled through the numbers, then stopped on the most recent, noting the San Antonio prefix. What in blazes was the kid up to? He didn't know whether to be angry or relieved that Josh wasn't calling from the Red Rock police department.

He could do a reverse lookup to find the number but it would be faster just to call it, he decided. He dialed and waited through six rings before somebody picked up.

"Yeah?" a smoker-rough, impatient-sounding female voice answered.

"Hey, my friend called me a little while ago from this pay phone and needed a ride but he forgot to give me an intersection to pick him up," he quickly lied. "Can you tell me where you're at?"

"Hang on. This ain't my usual stroll. I don't know this neighborhood. Just a sec." She returned a second later. "My friend says we're on the corner of Floyd Curl and Breezy Hill."

"Near the hospital?"

"Yeah. That's it. Hey, man, I think your friend might have found another set of wheels. Ain't nobody else here but us. You could give me a ride, though. Me and my friend can wait right here for you."

"You two might be waiting a while, sugar. But thanks anyway."

He hung up on her protests and found Julie watching him with a curious look in her eyes.

"That was quick thinking, to say you were picking up a friend."

He shrugged. "Old cop trick. I've got a million of them."

"I'm beginning to figure that out," she said. "We're going to go check it out, aren't we? Maybe we can find Josh's car somewhere in the vicinity."

"That's exactly what I was thinking. But you don't have to do this, Julie. I can handle things on my own."

"I know you can, but I'm worried about him, too."

She paused, looking uncertain for the first time all night. "If you would rather not have me along for whatever reason, I certainly can understand but I would like the chance to help if you want me."

"It's not that. I want you."

He heard the echo of his words and wished he could yank them back, but they hovered between them.

She cleared her throat. "That's good."

"I want you along," he corrected, trying not to be too obvious about amending his statement. "It's only that it's already past midnight and I know an all-nighter trip to the city wasn't in your plans for the evening."

"I can be flexible, Ross. We can keep each other awake."

Inappropriate images popped into his head and refused to leave there. He could think of far more enticing ways for the two of them to stay awake than looking for his recalcitrant nephew, but he knew those kinds of thoughts about Julie were dangerous.

He wanted to tell her to forget it, that he was better off on his own. But she had been wonderful all evening, helping him get into teen hangouts that otherwise might have been off-limits to him.

"All right," he said. "Let's go to San Antonio. It's a good thing we've already got all your provisions, isn't it? Looks like it might be a long night."

Three hours later, they were no closer to finding his nephew and Ross was beginning to wonder if they should even be looking. The kid was now officially three hours past eighteen. He was an adult. If he wanted to take off for a night, was Ross really in a position to have any objection?

Or even to worry about him?

Maybe he should have left Julie at the house in case Josh tried to call again. He had taken the precaution of changing the message on the answering machine, leaving pointed instructions for Josh to call Ross's cell phone immediately if he happened to call home and got the message, and they had left scrawled messages all over the house saying the same thing.

As Ross drove through some of the rougher neighborhoods of San Antonio, he worried he was putting Julie through all this unnecessarily.

He glanced over at the passenger seat. She was hanging on, but just barely. For the last half-hour, her lids had been drooping and her face was tight with fatigue.

"All right. I'd say we've tried long enough. We've covered a three-mile perimeter around the pay phone and come up empty. Let's get you back to Red Rock."

She scrambled up in the seat. "I'm sorry. No. I'm fine. Don't stop searching on my account."

"This is worse than looking for a needle in a haystack. We don't even know if the needle's here at all or in some other haystack altogether. You need a little rest. And to be honest, I could use some sleep myself."

She slanted him a look. "What would you do if I weren't here?"

"My apartment isn't far from here. Under other circumstances, I would probably catch a few hours of sleep there and head out again first thing."

"Let's do that, then. I can bunk on your couch. It's silly to drive all the way back to Red Rock if you're going to be here bright and early in the morning looking for Josh anyway."

Even for 3:00 a.m. logic, her words made sense. Beyond the time it would save in the morning, he wasn't sure she would make it all the way back to Red Rock.

And Josh was close. He sensed it somehow, with that cop's intuition that had never failed him yet. He had learned not to ignore it—even if that meant sharing his apartment for a few hours with Julie Osterman, the woman he had vowed to do his best to stay away from.

By the time they reached his place she was nearly asleep, but she managed to stumble out of his car and up the steps to his third-floor apartment.

He didn't know if it was the night air or the climb, but by the time they reached his door, a little color had returned to her cheeks and her eyes didn't look nearly as bleary.

As he unlocked the door and flipped on a light, he told himself the apprehension was completely his imagination.

She did a slow turn then walked to the window.

"Oh," she breathed.

"It's not much, I know."

"No, it's great! What an incredible view."

Though his apartment was only on the third floor, he overlooked the River Walk. His favorite evening activity was sitting out on the small terrace with a beer, enjoying the lights in the trees, the boats on the water and all the activity below.

He opened the sliding door and she walked out, lifting her face to the night air.

Though the lights of the city muted the stars much more than they did out in Red Rock, the heavens still offered an impressive display, a vast sea of tiny pinpricks of light against the black silk of the night sky.

Just a few hours before daylight, the River Walk was quiet now compared to how it probably had been even an hour or two ago.

"This is great. If I lived here, I would have a tough time wanting to do anything but sit here and enjoy."

She was beautiful, he thought. Lovely in that serene way that sometimes stole his breath.

And tougher than she looked, he admitted. She had stuck with him all evening, even through some of the rougher neighborhoods where he had looked for Josh. She hadn't shied away from situations that might have made her uncomfortable. Instead, she had been right there with him, keeping an eye out for his nephew.

And her provisions. He fought a smile all over again. How adorable was it that she had packed everything from his favorite cola to bandages, just in case?

"Come on," he said after a moment. "Let's get you settled. You can take the bedroom. I'll show you where everything is. I might even have an extra toothbrush."

She arched an eyebrow. Though she didn't say anything, he could read the speculation in her eyes.

"Josh comes to stay with me sometimes and he always seems to forget his so I try to pick up a few extras when I'm at the store."

He had no idea why he was compelled to defend himself but he didn't want her thinking he was in the habit of bringing strange women back to his apartment. He rarely even brought women who *weren't* strange here. The last time had been further back than he cared to remember.

He led the way down the hall to his bedroom, grateful he had taken time to pop over and clean up a bit just a few days ago, when he was in town catching up on things at the office.

"I'm sure I've got a T-shirt or something you can sleep in."

"Thanks. That would be great."

He opened a drawer and pulled out one of his less disreputable T-shirts and tossed it at her. She caught it one-handed and clutched it to her chest.

"Thank you."

She looked so soft and rumpled, with her hair a little bit messed from dozing in the car and her eyes wide and impossibly blue. As he gazed at her, she swallowed and offered a tremulous smile and his body burned with sudden, insatiable hunger.

Her smile slid from her features though she didn't look away, and he wondered if he was imagining the sudden tension, the swirls of awareness that seemed to eddy around them.

"I'm sorry to take your bed," she murmured.

"No problem. I don't mind the couch." His voice sounded raspy and tight. He cleared his throat. "Good night, then."

"I…good night."

He watched her for a few seconds more, then swallowed a groan and stepped forward. One kiss. Surely they could both survive one little kiss. It seemed a small enough thing when he had spent all night with her and managed to keep his hands to himself, when his body was crying out for so much more.

Chapter Eleven

With a breathy, sexy little moan that scorched down every nerve ending, she slid into his kiss as if she had been waiting all night for his mouth to find hers.

She tasted of coffee and something sweet and cinnamony and he couldn't get enough. He pulled her closer, relishing the soft curves against his chest and the way she wrapped her arms around his neck as if she couldn't bear to let him go.

He wanted more. He wanted *everything,* all of her gasps and the inhaled breaths and those infinitely arousing little sounds she made.

Her mouth was soft and luscious and so welcoming that he lost track of time. For several delectable moments, all the stresses weighing on his shoulders lifted away and the only thing that mattered to him was this woman, this moment.

He deepened the kiss, his tongue tangling with hers, and

he felt the little tremor that shook her body as she responded, heard the little hitch in her breathing. His body was rock hard in an instant and a slow, unsteady ache spread through him.

He slid a hand to her back, under her shirt, and the sultry softness of her skin against his fingers was irresistible.

One kiss wouldn't be enough.

How could it be, when he found just the small brush of her skin against his hands so heady, so addictive?

If he didn't stop now, though, he wasn't sure he would be able to find the strength. Even now, it took all his control to wrench his mouth from hers.

"We have to stop, Julie."

"Why?" she murmured against his mouth. He groaned at the note of genuine confusion in her voice.

"We don't…it's not…"

She kissed the corner of his mouth before he could form a single coherent thought and his brain took a siesta when, with tiny, silky little darts of her tongue, she began licking her way across to the other side.

"What were you saying?" she murmured, her voice low and husky.

"No idea," he answered truthfully, and returned the kiss with all the fierce hunger raging through him.

When she had walked into his apartment earlier, Julie had been emotionally drained and physically exhausted from their futile all-night search for Josh. But his kiss was as invigorating as a straight shot of high-octane caffeine.

Her body buzzed with heat and energy, like she was standing in a desert windstorm, being buffeted from every direction.

She had enough energy right now to run a marathon without even working up a sweat.

Or to spend what was left of the night in his arms.

She shivered as he trailed kisses down her jawline to the sensitive skin of her throat and then down to the open collar of her blouse.

Desire surged through her, wild and potent, as he pressed kisses to the curve of her breast above her bra. His mouth tasted her, exploring every inch he could reach that wasn't covered by her clothing, but it still wasn't enough.

Not nearly enough.

Her gaze held his as she shrugged out of her sweater and reached trembling fingers to unbutton her shirt.

His brown eyes blazed with desire as he watched her and she saw a little muscle jump in his cheek.

"Are you sure about this?" he asked, his voice little more than a growl. "We can still stop now, though it just might kill me."

"Absolutely sure," she replied. To prove it, she pulled her arms through the sleeves of her shirt, quickly worked the front clasps of her bra and then stepped out of her jeans.

The raw hunger in his eyes did crazy little things to her insides. She wasn't sure a man had ever looked at her like this, as if she was every fantasy he had ever conjured up.

She shivered a little at the force of that look but she didn't back away. How could she?

"Your turn," she murmured, and her hands found the buttons of his shirt, then his pants. She wasn't sure where this eager response was coming from but she liked it.

She had always enjoyed the closeness of making love with her husband in his better years, but it had been a long, long time for her. She couldn't remember this kind of urgent ache inside her, this insistent, undeniable need to be closer.

She had to touch him. All of him. He was masculine and

tough and his lean strength beckoned her, seduced her. She trailed her fingers across the planes of his chest, relishing his hard muscles and the leashed strength beneath her hands.

His abdominal muscles contracted tightly when she gently dipped her thumbs into the hollow below his ribcage and he stood immobile under her exploring touch for only a little longer before he groaned under his breath and pulled her against him again.

She didn't mind. He was warm and solid against her bare skin. As he kissed her, he pulled her close enough that her breasts were pressed against that hard chest she had been exploring earlier and she couldn't breathe around the delicious friction of her skin against his.

At last he lowered her to his bed and she could see the lights of the city spread out beyond his window. He had angled his bed to take full advantage of the view through the wide windows and somehow she found the idea of him lying in his bed looking out at the night sweetly charming.

And then she forgot all about the city lights and everything else but Ross when his mouth covered hers for another long, drugging kiss at the same time his hand found her breast, his fingers clever and arousing on the peak.

She gasped, arching into him. His thumb teased her nipple, rolling it around and around until she thought she would implode from the tension and the heat inexorably building inside her.

When he slid his mouth away from hers and lowered his head to her breasts, she nearly came off the bed from the torrent of sensations pouring through her. He teased and tasted for a long time, until she was writhing beneath him, desperate and aching for so much more.

At last, those deft fingers headed lower, toward the core

of her heat. She clutched him tightly, pressing her mouth to the warm column of his neck as his thumb danced across her thighs, coming close but not quite reaching the place she ached most for him to touch.

He circled around it and continued to tease until she finally growled with frustration and nipped at his shoulder.

His low laugh rang through the room. His gaze met hers and her heart seemed to swell at the lighthearted expression in his eyes, a side of Ross she rarely saw but which she was coming to adore.

"Very carnivorous of you, Ms. Osterman."

"I have my moments, when provoked," she answered, her voice husky.

"Remind me to provoke you more often, then," he murmured.

She smiled and he stared at her mouth for a long time, his expression unreadable and then he kissed her again, his mouth slow and unmistakably tender on hers.

Oh, she was in trouble here, she thought as heat began to build again, as he continued to tease her.

"Just touch me already," she all but begged.

He laughed roughly. "With pleasure. And I absolutely mean that."

His fingers finally found her and she cried out as she nearly climaxed with just one slight touch.

She thought she knew what to expect. She had been married for five years. Before her husband's illness, she had always considered their lovemaking fulfilling, an enriching, important part of their marriage.

This insatiable need for Ross was something completely out of her experience. She thought of that desert windstorm again, fierce and violent, ripping aside a lifetime of convention and restraint.

It frightened her more than a little, this lack of control, this urge to throw herself into the teeth of the maelstrom and let it carry her away.

She could feel herself begin to withdraw, to scramble back to the safety and security of that restraint, but Ross wasn't about to allow it.

"Let go," he whispered in her ear. "Let go for me, Julie."

His words were all it took to send her tumbling into the storm. He lifted her higher, higher, and then she cried out his name as she climaxed.

He quickly donned a condom from the bedside table and entered her even before the last tremor shook her body. His gaze locked with hers as his body joined hers, and she felt truly alive for the first time in forever.

She wanted to burn every sensation to memory—his scent, of cedar and sage and something citrusy she couldn't identify, the salty, masculine tang of his skin, his strength surrounding her, engulfing her. She wrapped her arms around him as tightly as she could manage.

He could hurt her.

The thought slithered into her mind out of nowhere and seemed to take hold, despite the hazy satisfaction still encompassing her.

She wasn't sure if she could treat this moment with the same casualness she knew Ross would. This meant something to her, something rare and precious and beautiful. She only hoped she could hold on to that and remember it as such after he pushed her away once more, as she was quite certain he would when the night was over.

That wild hunger began to climb inside her, insistent and demanding, and she pushed her concerns away. She would savor every moment with him. She wasn't going to ruin the magic and wonder of this moment with regret, with needless worry about the future.

With renewed enthusiasm, she threw herself into the kiss and after a surprised moment, he responded even more intensely.

His movements became more urgent, more demanding, and she arched to meet him, welcoming each joining of their bodies.

"Julie," he gasped after a long moment, and then he arched his back one more time as he found completion.

In the sweet, languid afterglow, she lay in his arms, trying to burn the memory into her mind. She couldn't regret this, even though she could already feel the tiny cracks in her heart expanding.

He would hurt her. She only hoped she was strong enough to endure it.

It was her last thought before she surrendered to the *other* demands of her body and finally slept.

Julie was beautiful in sleep. Her hair curled around her face in a filmy, sensuous cloud and long lashes fanned high cheekbones.

She looked delicate and lush at the same time and he couldn't seem to look away.

How could he ever have guessed a few short weeks ago that the prim and tight-lipped do-gooder he had thought her to be that night at the Spring Fling art fair would be so wildly passionate in bed?

He should have guessed it by the fierce way she defended the scruffy teenager he erroneously thought had been stealing her purse. He had been so busy snapping back at her that he hadn't allowed himself to see past her anger to the breathtakingly beautiful woman behind it.

She fell asleep as easily as a kitten in his bed and with the same liquid stretch of her limbs.

He pulled her closer and she purred and snuggled into him. It gave him the oddest feeling, this complete trust she had in him. He found it exhilarating and terrifying at the same time and wasn't quite sure how he should react.

Over her shoulder, he could see the lights in the trees outside on the River Walk. He watched them flicker and dance on the breeze, as he did many nights. This time his mind wasn't busy running through the details of a case. It was too occupied with Julie and the mass of contradictions she presented. She could be sweet one moment, fiery the next; pensive with one breath, then wildly passionate the next.

Everything about her fascinated him, from the courage she displayed after becoming a young widow under such tragic circumstances to the dedication she devoted to her job.

He thought of the huge basket of provisions she had packed earlier tonight and smiled all over again. It didn't last very long, though, when he suddenly remembered just why she had packed that basket.

Josh.

He hadn't thought of his nephew once in the last hour. Not once. Josh was out there somewhere, possibly in trouble, and Ross had forgotten all about him, simply because he found Julie so enticing.

He let out a breath, feeling chilled even though his bedroom was a comfortable temperature.

He needed to focus. He should never have given in to the hunger to kiss her. He was being pulled in too many different directions and right now his family needed him. He couldn't regret it, though. Not right now, with Julie warm and soft in his arms and this curiously appealing tightness in his chest.

He must have drifted asleep eventually. When he awoke, pale dawn sunlight was coyly peeking through the windows where he had forgotten to draw the curtains.

He stretched a little, struck by a curious feeling of contentment inside him. He wasn't used to it. In truth, the quiet peace of it left him a little unsettled and he didn't quite know how to react.

He gazed down at Julie, still sleeping beside him. If anything, she looked even lovelier than she had a few hours earlier.

Her mouth was slightly parted in sleep and she made a tiny, breathy little sound. He wanted to kiss her, with an acute, concentrated desperation.

He couldn't do it. It wouldn't be fair, not when she needed her sleep.

He tried to shift away but even his slight, barely perceptible movement must have disturbed her.

She blinked her eyes open and gazed at him for a moment, then she smiled softly and he had the random thought that the sun breaking across the city after weeks of rain couldn't be any more lovely or more welcome.

"Good morning," she murmured, her voice throaty and low.

"Hi."

"How long did we sleep?"

He glanced over at the digital readout on his alarm clock. "Not long enough. Only a few hours. It's almost six-thirty."

She reached her arms over her head and stretched until her fingers touched the headboard. "That's funny. I feel oddly invigorated."

He had the sudden, painful awareness that she was naked beneath the sheet that barely covered her. She was inches away from him, all that soft, glorious skin and those delectable curves.

His body snapped brightly to attention.

"Invigorated. Yeah. I know what you mean," he muttered.

She smiled again, her eyes half-lidded and knowing, and he couldn't mistake the sultry invitation. He held out as long as he could manage—oh, maybe a second and a half—before he lowered his head to hers and kissed her.

She responded just as sweetly as she had a few hours earlier, her mouth warm, slick and eager against his. Those arms she had just stretched out above her slid around his neck now and she pulled him close.

He loved when she touched him. Whether it was a casual hand on his arm in the middle of a conversation or her lips brushing his or her body arching against him in the sweet throes of passion, he couldn't seem to get enough of her.

A weird feeling seemed to trickle through him as that sensuous magic surrounded them again. It welled in his chest, clogged in his throat. Something warm and tender and terrifying. He wasn't sure what it might be—and he wasn't sure he liked it.

He wanted to take care of her. To cherish her. To rub her feet at the end of a hard day and make sure her car was filled with gasoline when she needed it and cook her fish on the grill just the way she liked it.

What was happening to him? For one jittery, panicky minute, Ross wanted to jump out of bed and rush out of his apartment and not look back. He didn't want this. Any of it. He didn't need another soul to take care of in his life, especially not a woman whose heart was so huge and full of love.

Anyway, she didn't need somebody else to watch out for her. She was doing fine on her own. She especially didn't need a cynical ex-cop with more baggage than an airline lost and found.

"Something wrong?" she asked, watching him carefully out of those big blue eyes, and he realized he had wrenched his mouth away and was staring at her as if she had just sat up in the bed and started spouting pig latin.

He quickly forced his emotions under control. He'd had plenty of practice at that when he was a kid and again as a cop.

This weird feeling wasn't love. It couldn't be. He wouldn't *let* it be.

He liked her well enough and he was more grateful than he could ever say for her help with Josh. That's all it was.

"What is it?" she asked.

"Nothing. Nothing at all," he said.

He pushed away the jumpy feeling and turned his attention to that spot on her neck that he had discovered drove her crazy. She shivered and tightened her arms around him.

He might have thought their second time making love wouldn't have been as intense, as shattering, as the first. He knew what to expect, after all. He had already had the exhilarating chance to explore all those delectable curves. He had already discovered that little mole above her hipbone and he knew she made those soft, sexy little sounds when she was close to finding release.

But if anything, the repeat performance was even more astonishing. It was slower-paced, sweeter somehow, as if they were moving through soft, warm honey. Every sensation seemed magnified a hundredfold. He had never known a woman to give herself so generously, without any reservations, and it stunned and humbled him.

Even more, she acted just as stunned by her own response, which only seemed to accentuate his own.

She cried out his name when she climaxed, then wrapped

her arms tightly around him when he joined her with a groan, and Ross never wanted her to let go.

All those scary feelings crowded back as he held her afterward, her head nestled in the crook of his shoulder, but he forced himself to hold them all back.

He *wasn't* in love with her. No way, he told himself.

He was still trying to convince himself of that when his cell phone suddenly bleated from somewhere in the bedroom.

Chapter Twelve

He might have been tempted to ignore it, to dive back into the heat and magic they shared, if not for the sudden recollection of just why they were there in his apartment in San Antonio.

But who else would be calling him at 7:00 a.m., unless Josh had just bothered to return to the house and found all his strongly worded orders to do just that?

"Is it Josh?" Julie asked.

"It had better be," he muttered. He grabbed his phone from the bedside table.

"Where the hell are you?"

A long silence met his growled question and then a small female voice spoke. "Um, still at the jail. But my lawyer assures me that's only for another few hours. They're releasing me on my own recognizance."

"Frannie?" He scrambled up against the headboard and

pulled the comforter up to his waist, as if his sister could see through the telephone.

"What are you talking about?" he demanded. "What's going on? Why are you calling me so early?"

She let out a strangled sound that was half sob, half laugh.

"You haven't heard, I guess. Nobody has picked up the story yet this morning since the police aren't releasing any details. They're letting me go."

"Dropping the charges?"

"The next best thing to it, my attorney says. They've dropped my bail to nothing. They're not holding me any longer. I'm going to be freed, Ross. Can you believe it? They've brought someone else in for questioning. I'm going home to Josh. It's like some kind of miracle, isn't it?"

His sister started crying in earnest but Ross felt as if his heart had jerked to an abrupt stop.

He couldn't believe it. He didn't *want* to believe it. But how could it possibly be a coincidence that Josh goes missing a few hours ago "helping out a friend" at the same time somebody gets hauled in for questioning about killing Lloyd?

Josh, what the hell have you done?

But, maybe he was way off base. If Josh had confessed and was now in custody, wouldn't Frannie be hysterical instead of reacting to the news with this sort of stunned jubilation?

"Who killed him?" he asked, unable to keep the wariness from his voice but hoping she didn't notice.

"I don't know. Nobody's telling me anything," she answered. "All I know is that they've got some 'person of interest' and they're ready to let me go. Oh, I can't wait to be home. Will you come get me?"

He slid out of the bed, already reaching for his khakis. "Of course. Stay in touch and call me the minute you hear from your attorney. I'll be there as soon as I can."

"Don't wake up Josh, okay? I want to surprise him."

Ross frowned. Somebody in the family was definitely in for a surprise. He could only hope it was indeed Josh who was surprised at learning his mother had been released and not him and Frannie when they found Josh already in custody.

"I'll see you in a little while," he said, instead of responding to his sister's plea about her son.

He hung up, his mind racing in a hundred different directions as he yanked on his socks and thrust his arms through the sleeves of his shirt.

"Ross, what's going on?"

He looked toward the bed and found Julie watching him with consternation. How could he have forgotten Julie? She looked soft and tousled, her hair messed and her lips swollen from his mouth. He gazed at her, wishing with everything inside him that things could be different, that he could stay with her, right here in this warm, cozy bed.

But his family needed him. And just like always, he had no choice but to help. Still, the choice had never seemed so damned hard before.

"I've got to hurry back to Red Rock. That was Frannie."

Her features tightened with concern. "What is it?"

"They're letting her go. They've brought someone else in for killing Lloyd Fredericks."

She stared at Ross, not quite sure she had heard him correctly. "Letting her go? Are you serious?"

"Completely." He started buttoning up his cotton shirt and it was only as she watched his grim features that Julie realized why all this seemed so discordant and unreal. He wasn't reacting like a man who had just learned his sister was about to be freed from jail.

"Okay, my brain obviously isn't working correctly yet this morning," she said. "Tell me again why you're not throwing the world's biggest party? Isn't this what you've wanted? What you've been working so hard to bring about for the last two weeks? Frannie's coming home, Ross! Why on earth do you look like you're heading to a funeral, instead of celebrating?"

He was silent as he started to slip on his boots, but his features looked even more austere than normal.

"Ross, tell me. What's wrong?"

At last he lifted his gaze to hers and she nearly gasped at the haunted expression in his brown eyes. Her mind sifted through the pieces, Frannie, Lloyd, the Spring Fling and the events of that awful night.

And Josh.

Josh was the missing piece, she realized, as everything clicked into place. She thought of his determined efforts to find his nephew the night before, and the odd phone call he had made to the police station, their seemingly casual route back to the Frederickses' home that had led them right past the station house.

She gasped and stared at him. "You think it's Josh they've hauled in. You think he killed his father!"

He didn't respond for a long moment but his silence was answer enough. "I don't know what I think," he finally said. "All I know is that Josh fought bitterly with his father that night and uttered what could be taken as a direct threat. He was seen with the murder weapon, not long before his father's body was found. He knows something, something he's not saying. I told you that since the murder, he's been secretive.

He takes these mysterious phone calls and I can tell he's troubled."

"He's had a rough few weeks, losing his father and his mother at once. You can't honestly think he had anything to do with killing Lloyd! That he would let his mother go to jail for his own crime!"

"Where is he then?"

She had no answer to give him, though she fervently wished she did.

"I'm sorry about this," Ross said, "but I've got to go back to Red Rock right away. I can drop you off at your house on the way."

"Okay. I only need a moment." She rose and quickly began to dress again, thinking with regret of the brief, stolen time they had shared together. Something told her those moments were as elusive and rare as a wildflower growing on a harsh, unforgiving rock face.

As she dressed, she listened to his one-sided conversation with the police station. She could have guessed the outcome, even before he hung up the phone in disgust.

"They're not saying anything until charges are officially filed, which might or might not happen any moment. I need to haul out of here."

"Of course." She threw on her blouse and sweater, doing her best to block out the dull ache of regret.

"I need to make some phone calls on the way back to Red Rock to see if I can find out what the hell is going on, just who it is who's confessed. How do you feel about taking the wheel so I'm not distracted by talking while I drive?"

"Anything I can do to help. You know I want to do whatever I can."

"Thanks."

Though gratitude flashed in his gaze, it was quickly gone, replaced by a deep anxiety. She wanted to soothe it but she knew nothing she said would help him right now. But she could do as he asked and take at least one responsibility from his wide shoulders by driving them back to Red Rock.

He must have spoken with a half-dozen people as she took the shortest route possible away from San Antonio. Listening to him probe each contact for information was fascinating. He seemed to know exactly the right buttons to push with every person he spoke with. He could be brash and abrasive when necessary, but he could also pull out unexpected wiles that completely charmed her—and whoever he was talking to.

As they neared the Red Rock town limits, she listened to him try to skillfully pry information out of a source in the police department.

"You're not holding out on me, are you, Loraine?" he asked after a short conversation where he had exhibited a delicate finesse that surprised her.

He was quiet for a moment and Julie would have given anything to know what the person on the other end of the line was saying.

"How sure are you on that?" he asked after a long moment, his features unreadable. "Ninety-nine. That's good. And the other one percent?"

Loraine said something that made him laugh. When the worry left his features, even for a moment, he looked younger, lighter. Almost happy.

She jerked her gaze back to the road, her heart tumbling around in her chest like a bingo ball in the chute.

She was in love with him.

The knowledge burrowed into her heart, as clear as the exit

sign on the freeway. She wanted to push it away, to deny and disclaim, but she couldn't. She knew exactly what this dangerous tenderness curling through her meant.

She was in love with Ross Fortune, a hard and cynical man who seemed the last one on earth she ought to fall for, a man who was an expert at protecting himself from any deeper emotions.

She loved him. His deep core of decency, the care and concern he doled out to his family, his complete commitment to doing what was right.

She loved him—and he so desperately needed someone to love him, even if he would never admit it.

Why did that someone have to be her? she wondered with grim fatalism. She didn't want to love him. She wanted to go back to the way things had been just a few short weeks ago, before he had barreled into her life.

He would hurt her.

The knowledge hovered around her like the wavy mirages on the highway. Pain, harsh and unforgiving and unavoidable, waited for her. He would hurt her and she could do absolutely nothing to hold it back.

The time for protecting her heart might have been before that fateful night when he had accused poor Marcus Gallegos of stealing. She had been heading for this moment, for this inevitable pain, since then.

She might have been able to reduce its severity if she had walked away after that evening, if she had maintained all her careful defenses. Instead, she had let her life become entwined with his through Josh. Each time she saw Ross, she had allowed him to sneak a little further past her defenses.

Tears burned behind her eyes, blurring the road in front of her, but she blinked them away. He hadn't hurt her yet. She refused to waste this particular moment in anticipation of the future pain she knew was on the way.

He ended the call a moment later and Julie knew she wasn't mistaken that his mood seemed lighter. His eyes seemed brighter, his expression less anxious.

"That was a friend of mine who works in central booking at the jail. She said the guy they're holding is a 40-year-old male."

"So not Josh."

Her voice sounded like she'd just swallowed a handful of gravel but she hoped he didn't notice or that he would attribute it to an emotional reaction to the news of his nephew's apparent reprieve.

"I won't be completely convinced of that until I find the little bugger and figure out where he's been all night. But no, at this point it looks like somebody else in Lloyd's legion of enemies had it in for him."

"How tragic, that so many people in Red Rock could have enough motive to want a man dead."

When he said nothing for several moments, she glanced away from the road just long enough to catch the quizzical look he threw at her.

She flushed, her hands tightening on the steering wheel. "Why are you looking at me like that?"

"You didn't even know Lloyd, did you?"

She shook her head.

"You didn't know the man but as far as I can tell, you're the only one besides his own mother and his mistress who finds anything to mourn in his death."

"I just think it's terribly sad that someone could take the precious gift of life and all the opportunities given him to make the world a better place and then twist them all so hideously that most of the world is glad he's gone."

He reached across the width of the seat and picked up her hand. Before she quite realized what he intended, he lifted her fingers and pressed his mouth to the back of her hand, in a very un-Ross-like gesture.

"Do you know what your greatest gift is?" he asked.

She let out a shaky breath, wondering how on earth she was going to collect the tattered pieces of herself when this was over. "What?"

"You make everyone around you want to be better. To try harder to see the world through those same bright, optimistic eyes."

She loved the feel of his hand holding hers, the safety and warmth of him, even as she wanted to snatch her hand away, to protect herself from any more encroachment on her heart.

"You didn't get nearly enough sleep last night if you can wax philosophical this morning."

"No, I didn't."

Heat scorched through her at his words as she remembered all the ways they had kept each other awake in the night. She was almost positive she was able to keep her fingers from trembling in his.

"Do you mind if we swing by Frannie's house before I drop you off? I want to make sure Josh hasn't checked in. For all we know, he could be asleep in his own bed, not knowing that everything has suddenly changed."

"No problem," she answered, trying not to be too disappointed when he released her hand so she could use both of hers for driving.

Ross must have been listening to his cop's intuition again. The very moment she pulled into the Frederickses' driveway, a battered yellow sports car pulled up beside them and Josh climbed out.

He looked tired, Julie thought. Tired and worried and somehow older than he had appeared the last time she saw him.

She wondered how he would react to seeing them together so early at this time of the day but he didn't so much as raise an eyebrow.

"Hi," he said when they joined him outside their respective vehicles. "You two are out and about early this morning."

Already the morning was shaping up to be a warm one. But the sun-warmed heat was nothing compared to the anger suddenly radiating from Ross.

"Well?" he snapped to his nephew. "Let's hear your explanation? I'll warn you, it better be good."

Josh looked genuinely bewildered and a bit wary. She also thought she saw a little guilt there, as well. "Explanation for what?"

"For what?" Ross's voice rose on the last word. "Let's start with where the hell you've been all night. Julie and I drove around Red Rock and San Antonio half the night looking for you!"

His eyes widened with shock. "Why? I left you a note and then I called and left a message on voice mail. Didn't you get it?"

"Sure we got your note," Ross answered tightly. "Do you think you could try to be a bit less cryptic next time? We didn't know *what* was going on. And then when you didn't answer your blasted phone all night long, what were we supposed to think?"

"I told you a friend of mine needed help." Josh suddenly seemed as taut and angry as his uncle and Julie wondered how much of his reaction was due to fatigue.

"Did it ever once occur to you that saying only 'a friend needs help' could mean anything from algebra homework to changing a flat tire to running drugs across the border? You said you were going to help this friend but you didn't say anything about it taking you the whole damn night."

"I didn't expect to take all night. It was a…routine thing. But there were…complications. But everything's okay now. She…everything's okay."

An echo of worry flickered in his eyes and Julie reached a hand to rest on his arm. "Are you sure everything's okay, Josh? You look tired."

Josh's gaze met hers and for an instant that illusion of maturity disappeared and he looked suddenly desperately young. He seemed to want to lean on someone. He opened his mouth and she held her breath, hoping he would choose to confide in her and his uncle, but then he changed his mind and closed it again.

He straightened his shoulders. "Yeah. It's been a long night. Sounds like for you guys, too. I'm really sorry you made an unnecessary trip to San Antonio, but you can't blame me for your own overreaction. I told you not to worry or wait up. And I left you a message, too. I told you not to worry about me."

"Easy for you to say!"

"I'm officially eighteen, Uncle Ross. An adult in the eyes of the law. You don't have to treat me like a baby and run off and look for me like some kind of bounty hunter."

Ross looked angry and uncomfortable at the same time. Julie cut him off before he could voice the angry words forming in his eyes and possibly say something he might come to regret after their respective tempers had cooled.

"We were worried about you," she said to Josh. "It seems uncharacteristic for you to just take off like this."

He suddenly seemed inordinately fascinated with the bluebells growing in his mother's flower garden. "It was an emergency. And that's all I can tell you right now."

Ross knew his nephew was holding out on him. The boy—no, not a boy anymore—had secrets in his eyes. Ross was an expert at extracting information from unwilling subjects and sifting through lies and subterfuge to the truth but somehow none of his techniques seemed to work on his nephew.

That was what happened when he let his emotions overrule his good sense. He ought to sit Josh in a room and make the kid tell him what was going on. But Josh was right, he was eighteen and Ross supposed he was entitled to a few secrets.

He was so relieved that Josh hadn't been involved with his father's murder that he supposed he could let the mystery of his whereabouts overnight remain just that for now—a mystery.

"If your cell phone had been working, I might have been able to call you to tell you the news," he said.

"What news?" Josh asked, his hand on the open door-frame of Ross's SUV.

He paused. "Your mom is being released from jail any minute now. I'm on my way to get her."

Josh stared at him as if he had just announced they were flying to Saturn later. "What?" he exclaimed. "Why didn't you say so?"

"You just got here. We haven't exactly had much time to chat."

"This is huge! What happened? Did the stupid district attorney finally agree to reduce her bail?"

"She's being let out on her own recognizance. According to my sources, they've got someone else they like for the murder."

He watched his nephew's reaction carefully and saw a

mix of emotions chase across his features, everything from shock to disbelief and finally a deep, pure relief.

"Who did they bring in?"

"I'm still trying to get answers to that. Your mom called me a little while ago and said her attorney was working on getting the charges against her dropped but she didn't know many details. I've been able to find out a little but not a name or anything like that. I'm heading down to the police station right now to see what else I can find out."

Josh's hand tightened on the doorframe. "I'm coming with you."

His nephew had obviously been up all night, judging by the fatigue lining his eyes and the heavy sag of his shoulders. But he was young enough to survive an all-nighter. Ross had a feeling he wouldn't be able to keep Josh away.

"Get in, then. We can drop Julie off at her place on the way."

He took over behind the wheel from Julie and she slid into the passenger seat beside him. The three of them were mostly silent on the five-minute drive to her house. Ross found himself grateful for the buffer of Josh's presence, suddenly aware of the monumental shift in his relationship with Julie after the night they had shared.

He wasn't ready for things to change. He enjoyed her friendship too much to ruin things with sex but he was afraid that's exactly what he had done.

He didn't want things to get messy with her but he knew with brutal self-awareness that he sucked at relationships. He was much better at short-term flings, where women had few expectations beyond a few dates and a good time.

Julie wasn't like that. As he pulled up to her small, tidy house near the elementary school, he could see the proof of it.

He walked around and opened her door—manners instilled in him by his uncles. He walked her to the front door, past colorful terra-cotta containers full of bright flowers and a trio of birdhouses.

This was just the sort of house that made him nervous. The flower gardens spoke of settling in, of commitment and permanence, all the things that seemed so foreign to him. He couldn't remember a single plant his mother had tried to grow. They had never been in one place long enough to see a seedling sprout anyway, so why bother?

He had been in his condo for five years, though. Why hadn't he ever tried to grow anything on the patio? He had perfect light out there and it wouldn't be a big deal to plant some tomatoes and maybe a pepper plant or two.

At her door, he paused, feeling intensely awkward, in light of all they had shared together the last few hours. She seemed to sense it, too, and fiddled with her purse and the keys she had used to unlock the door.

He struggled for something to say but everything sounded lame. *Thanks for the most incredible night of my life* sounded like it came right off the pathetic bachelor's morning-after playlist.

"Let me know what happens with Frannie, okay?" Julie finally said.

"I'll be sure to do that," he answered. His chest ached a little as the morning sun lit a halo around her. She looked as pretty and bright as her flower gardens and he knew she wasn't for him.

He was going to have to break things off with her. She was digging in too deep and he couldn't let her. Not when she scared the hell out of him.

He hated being one of Those Guys, who slept with a

woman and then brushed her off, especially when he had a feeling she expected more. But he also wasn't willing to string her along, not when he already was coming to care far too much for her.

Chapter Thirteen

Ross's heart ached in his chest. He wanted nothing but to pull her against him and hold on forever, which was more than enough reason to push her away.

"Julie, I…"

She shook her head and for just a moment, he thought he saw something like sorrow flicker there before it was quickly gone. "Ross, don't say anything. What happened earlier was…wonderful. We both wanted it to happen. But I completely understand that it was only a one-time thing."

He scratched his cheek. "Twice, technically."

She laughed roughly, though again he thought he saw regret in those soft blue eyes. "Okay, twice. My point remains that I don't expect anything more than that. You can put your mind at ease. I promise, I'm not going to be clingy or throw a scene or rush inside my house and cry for hours. Don't worry about me, okay?"

He should be relieved. Wasn't this what he wanted? So why did his chest continue to ache like he'd been punched?

"I'm not the kind of man you need, Julie. I wish I could be. You have no idea how much I wish I could be. But I'm not."

"How did you become such an expert on what I need?"

"It's my job to understand people. I have to be able to read things about people that even they don't always see. I have to be able to understand their motivations, their triggers, their personality types."

"And what's my personality type?"

She asked the question with deceptive casualness but he heard the sudden tightness in her voice, in the way she compressed her lips just a little too hard on the last consonant so it popped. He was in quicksand here, he suddenly sensed.

He glanced at the car where Josh watched them curiously, too far away, thank the Lord, to hear their conversation.

He didn't want to get into all this right now. But he had started things and he owed it to her to finish.

"You're a nurturer. A natural healer. You take people who are hurting and broken and you try to fix them. It's what you do with the kids you work with at the Fortune Foundation but I've seen you put the same effort into everyone. I saw you slip more than a few bills to anybody who looked like they had a sob story last night while we were looking for Josh."

A tiny muscle flexed in her check. "And you don't want to be healed."

He bristled. "I'm not broken."

"Aren't you?"

Her psychoanalytical put-the-question-back-on-the-poor-patient crap suddenly bugged the hell out of him.

"I'm fine," he snapped. "Absolutely fine. I've got everything I need."

She said nothing, only continued to study him out of those eyes that saw entirely too much.

"Everything was going just great in my life until two weeks ago when somebody whacked my brother-in-law. Now that they've found whoever it was who did it and Frannie's coming home, I can return to the life I had before and everything will get back to normal."

"In my business, we call that self-delusion."

"Call *what* self-delusion?"

"You're supposed to be an expert on figuring out what makes everybody else tick. Their motivations, their triggers, their personality types. Isn't that what you said? Can you really be so blind to your own?"

"What's that supposed to mean?"

"Nothing. Never mind. Goodbye, Ross."

She opened the door and though he knew Josh and Frannie waited for him, he couldn't help himself. He followed her inside.

"Tell me what you meant," he growled.

She studied him for a long moment, then she sighed. "You keep everyone away, don't you? Because of the instability of your childhood, you're so determined not to count on anybody else, to be so completely self-sufficient now that you're an adult, that you close off everybody except your family. Frannie and Josh. And even then, you feel like you have to shoulder every burden for them, not share a single worry. As a result, you're probably the most lonely man I've ever met."

He stared at her, thunderstruck by the harsh analysis. Her words sliced at him with brutal efficiency. How did she know anything about his childhood? Fast on the heels of the shock and hurt came the sharp flare of anger. She had no right to think she could sum up his world in a few neat little sentences.

"I take back everything I said," he snapped. "You're not a nurturer. You're just plain crazy. I'm absolutely not lonely. Hell, I can't get people to leave me alone long enough for me to be lonely!"

"I guess we can both be wrong about each other, then," she said, sounding so damn calm and reasonable, he wanted to punch something.

"I guess so. Better to find out now then sometime in the future after we've invested more than just a night with each other."

"I'm sure you're right," she murmured. "You'd better go, hadn't you? Your sister's waiting for you."

He gazed at her for a moment, wondering how this whole thing had taken such a wrong turn, then he nodded. "Yeah. I guess I'll see you around, then."

She only smiled that impassive smile at him and opened the door, leaving him no choice but to stalk through it and down the sidewalk.

Julie watched Ross drive away, his white SUV suddenly anything *but* unobtrusive as its tires spit gravel and careened around the corner.

Apparently he couldn't wait to get away from her.

Drat the man. She swiped at a tear trickling down the side of her nose and then another and another, grateful at least that she had the strength of will to hold them back until he was out of sight.

She wanted to rant and rave at Ross Fortune's stubborn self-protectiveness, his apparent willingness to walk away from the magic and wonder they had shared, just so that he could guard his psyche.

A good tantrum would at least be an outlet for the wild torrent of emotions damming up inside her, but the hardest thing to accept was that none of this was Ross's fault.

She walked into bed with him with her eyes open. She might not have consciously admitted she was already in love with him but deep down she must have known, just as she had to have realized somewhere inside that Ross was completely unavailable to her, at least emotionally.

She had convinced herself she was strong enough to live in the moment, to seize the chance to be with him without regrets or recriminations later.

What a fool she was. And she called *him* self-deluded! How could she have ever believed she could share that intimacy with him, let him inside her soul and not feel battered and bruised when he walked away from all she was willing to offer?

This was goodbye then.

Their respective worlds weren't likely to intersect again. With his sister on her way to freedom, Ross had no reason to stick around Red Rock. Frannie would be able to care for Josh from now on and accompany him to the Fortune Foundation for counseling sessions if he still needed them.

Ross would return to San Antonio and his private investigation practice and that lovely, impersonal apartment and his self-contained life that struck her as immeasurably sad.

She pressed her hands to her face for just a moment then dropped them to her knees. She would survive a broken heart. She had no choice. As Ross said, she was a healer, a nurturer, and she couldn't do any of that if she turned inside herself and wallowed in her own pain.

* * *

He was an ass.

Ross sat in the reception area of the police station, replaying his conversation with Julie over and over in his head.

Had he really called her crazy? He burned with chagrin just thinking about it. He had reacted like some kind of little kid, lashing out first to protect himself from being wounded by her words.

She deserved better from him than that. Julie had always been nothing but warm and kind to him. She had just spent the entire night helping him look for Josh, for hell's sake. And then when she gave him an opinion that *he* had solicited, he snapped back at her like a cornered grizzly. It was unfair and unnecessarily hurtful.

He had to make it right, somehow, but he had no idea where to start.

He still didn't buy what she was selling. He had moved past his childhood a long time ago. Yeah, he might still have scars. The insecurity of growing up with Cindy Fortune would have been rough on any kid, he wouldn't deny that. But he didn't dwell on it anymore. He hadn't for a long time.

And lonely. She said he was lonely. He didn't buy that, either. He had plenty of friends, good ones. They went to basketball games together and had barbecues and fishing trips out on his boat.

Okay, he would admit she was right that he didn't let too many people close. But that didn't mean he was some kind of freaking hermit.

He thought of the nights alone in his apartment when he would stand at the window gazing down at the River Walk, at the lights and the activity and the people walking together, content and happy in their tidy little family units.

More often than not, he would attribute the nameless ache inside him as he watched them to heartburn. It sure wasn't loneliness. Was it?

"Ross? You in there?"

He glanced up to find Josh staring at him with a quizzical look.

"Sorry. Did you say something?"

Josh rolled his eyes. "Only about a dozen times. I asked if I could borrow your cell phone to check on my friend."

The same friend whose troubles had occupied him all night? Ross wondered. He wanted to push his nephew to finally come clean and explain what was going on. But since he had screwed everything else up this morning, he decided maybe he ought to keep his mouth shut for now.

He handed over his phone and wasn't surprised when Josh walked outside to make his call. More secrets. He was getting pretty sick of them all.

Despite the fact that Frannie was to be released any moment now, Ross still didn't know much more than when she called him two hours before.

Try as he might, he couldn't manage to worm more information out of anyone in the department except what he already knew. A forty-year-old man was the new suspect in Lloyd's death.

He didn't understand why everyone was being so closed-mouthed about the whole thing, but he could guess. They were no doubt engaged in the age-old police game of CYA. Cover Your Ass. No doubt they realized they had rushed to judgment with Frannie without looking around for any other suspects and wanted to avoid making the same mistake again and possibly jeopardizing their case.

He didn't care who killed Lloyd, as long as it meant his

sister could return home where she belonged and he could go back to San Antonio where *he* belonged.

Josh returned a few moments later and handed his phone back.

"Everything okay with Lyndsey?" Ross hazarded a guess.

"Yeah, she's doing tons bet—" *Better.* Josh cut his word off but Ross completed the word for himself, even as his nephew frowned at being tricked into revealing more information than he wanted.

"What happened to her?" Ross asked. "Has she been sick?"

For an instant, he thought Josh would confide in him. He opened his mouth and Ross sensed he wanted to tell someone whatever was bothering him. Ross sat forward with an encouraging look, but before Josh could say anything, the door leading to the jail opened.

He and Josh both turned to look and found Frannie standing in the doorway, looking frail and exhausted, with no makeup and her blond hair scraped back in a ponytail.

Despite the outward signs of fatigue, her eyes glowed with joy.

"Josh. Oh sweetheart."

Josh rose from his seat, stumbled forward and then swept his mother into his arms. Both of them were crying a little, even his tough-guy, eighteen-year-old nephew. Ross watched their reunion, aware of a niggle of envy at the love the two of them shared, a love with no conditions or caveats.

Josh had probably never spent one moment wondering at his place in his mother's heart. Frannie loved him with everything she had.

Frannie touched Josh's face as if she couldn't quite believe he was there in front of her and then after a moment she remembered Ross and turned to hug him, as well. She felt like nothing more than fragile bones.

"You're fading away, Frannie," he growled. "Have you been on some kind of hunger strike in here?'

She shook her head. "I just…I haven't been very hungry. It was too hard to drum up an appetite when I could only think about how afraid I was."

If you were so blasted afraid, why didn't you defend yourself? Who were you covering for? Ross wanted to rail at his sister but he knew this wasn't the time. "We need to get you out of here and get some good cooking into you. What do you say we stop at Red on the way home for a huge brunch? We'll break out the champagne."

"That sounds delicious." She gave him a tremulous smile just as Loraine Fitzsimmons walked through.

"Hey, Ross." She smiled.

"Hi, Loraine. Thanks for the information earlier."

She looked around to make sure no one else could overhear them.

"Just thought I'd give you a heads up. They're questioning him again."

"Who is it?"

She cast another furtive look at the doorway. "You're not going to believe this. It's one of Mendoza boys. Says here it's Roberto. Isn't he the one who's been living in Denver?"

Ross had just half a second to wonder why the man had hated Lloyd enough to kill him and to entertain the possibility of trying to post bail for the guy, whoever he might be, when suddenly he was aware of Frannie's small sound of distress. A moment later his sister's eyes fluttered back in her head and she started to fall.

"Mom!" Josh exclaimed. He dived for her and though he

wasn't in time to catch her completely, he slowed the momentum of her fall.

Josh lowered her to the carpet and both he and Ross knelt over her.

Loraine hovered over them, her eyes wide with shock. "Do you want me to call a medic?" she asked.

"Give us a minute," Ross said. Frannie had looked so weak when she came out. Was it any wonder she had succumbed to exhaustion and nerves and fainted?

"Come on, Frannie. Come on back, sis."

"Come on, Mom," Josh added his voice. "You're scaring us."

She blinked her eyes open, then a moment later she scrambled to sit and looked around, trying to regain her bearings.

"Are you all right?" Ross asked. Her pulse seemed a little thready to him and he wondered if he ought to let Loraine go ahead and call a medic.

Frannie blinked a few more times, then her gaze met Loraine's and Ross saw full awareness come back in a rush. Frannie tried to stand but couldn't make it to her feet without his help.

"Take it easy," he said, but Frannie seemed to barely hear him.

"Who did you say they're holding?" she asked Loraine, and Ross couldn't miss the sudden urgency in her voice.

"Mendoza. Roberto Mendoza."

Frannie inhaled a ragged breath and, for a moment, Ross was afraid she would pass out again. "Do you know the guy?" he asked.

"I…no."

She was lying. No doubt about it. Frannie had always been a lousy liar. Maybe that was why she had opted instead to keep her mouth shut when she had been accused of killing her husband.

He knew most of the Mendozas on a casual basis, mostly because they were good friends with his family here in Red Rock. He tried to remember if he had ever met Roberto Mendoza and had a vague memory of bumping into the guy years ago on one of his visits to Red Rock.

What was his relationship with Frannie?

He was royally sick of all these Fortune family secrets. Though he wanted to drag his sister to one of the interview rooms in the police station until he got to the bottom of all this, he knew this wasn't the time. This should be a celebration for Frannie, a chance for her to start taking back her life.

As soon as things settled down for his sister, his own life could get back to normal. To stakeouts and paperwork and catching up on cases. He would be far too busy to pay any attention to those moments standing at his window in San Antonio, watching life go on below without him.

Chapter Fourteen

He really disliked weddings, even when they were family obligations.

A week after Frannie's release from jail, Ross stood in the extensive gardens at the Double Crown watching his cousin Darr dance with his very pregnant bride of less than an hour, Bethany Burdett. Bethany Burdett Fortune, now, he supposed.

It was a lovely evening for a wedding. Little twinkly lights had been strung through all the trees and the garden smelled sweet, like flowers and springtime.

Darr beamed with pride and his new wife looked completely radiant. That was what they said about pregnant women and brides—and since she qualified on both counts, Ross figured *radiant* was an accurate description. She also couldn't seem to take her eyes off Darr.

The two of them seemed deliriously happy together, he

would give them that. He hoped things would work out for the two of them and for Bethany's kid, which wasn't Darr's—and nobody was making a secret about it. The baby needed a dad and Darr appeared more than willing to step up and take responsibility. Ross just hoped he didn't grow to resent raising another man's kid.

They wouldn't have an easy road—a cynical thought to have just moments after their wedding, he knew, and he was slightly ashamed of himself for even entertaining it.

How did he get to be so pessimistic about happily-ever-afters? He couldn't really say he'd never seen a good marriage at work. His uncle William had adored his wife Molly before her death and they had been married for decades. Lily and Ryan had known several happy years, too, before Ryan's surprising death.

He couldn't deny there were many couples in his extended family who, by all appearances, had good, fulfilling marriages. He didn't begrudge any of them their joy, he just figured maybe Cindy's particular branch of the Fortune family tree had picked up some sort of withering disease that blighted their prospects of happy endings.

His mother had never stayed with any man for longer than a year or so. His brothers didn't seem capable of settling down, and God knows, his sister's marriage had been a farce from the beginning.

He glanced toward Frannie, sitting at a table with their cousin Nicholas and his fiancée Charlene. She looked as if she were only half-listening to their conversation and he wondered again why she didn't seem more ecstatic about being released from jail. She still seemed thin and withdrawn and she evaded and equivocated whenever he tried to probe about why she hadn't defended herself in Lloyd's murder and her strange reaction to finding out one of the Mendozas had confessed to it.

Something was up with her and it bugged him that she still refused to tell him what was going on, even after all they had been through the past month. She was a grown woman, though. If she didn't want to tell him what was troubling her, he couldn't force her.

He glanced at his watch, wondering if twenty minutes into the reception counted as fulfilling his familial obligation so he could go. When he looked up, his heart seemed to catch his throat when he saw Julie Osterman walk into the garden, wearing a soft yellow dress that made her look as if she had brought all the sunshine along with her.

In the week since he had left her at her house with such heated words, he had forgotten how breathtaking she was, with that soft brown hair shot through with blonde and those incredible blue eyes and delicate features. He suddenly realized with some vexation that if he had the chance, he would be quite content just to stand there and gawk at her all night.

As if she felt him watching her, she shifted her attention from her conversation with his cousin Susan and looked up. For a long moment, the two of them just stared at each other, their gazes locked. Emotions swelled up inside him, thick and heavy and terrifying. He saw something in her eyes, something that made them look huge and liquid and sad, and then she deliberately turned back to answer something Susan said to her, though he knew she was still aware of him, of this strange bond tugging between them.

He wanted fiercely to go to her. His chest ached and he actually lifted a hand to rub at it then caught himself and shoved it into the pocket of his dress slacks instead. It still throbbed though, an actual physical ache that made him feel slightly ridiculous.

He had missed her. More than he had ever dreamed possible. In the week since he had seen her—since those stunning few hours they had shared at his apartment in San Antonio—she hadn't been out of his mind for long. Everything seemed to remind him of her, from shooting hoops with Josh to the starlit view from his bedroom window at night to—of all silly things—the scent of the particular brand of fabric softener he used, just because that day in the grocery store he had talked to her while they were standing in the laundry aisle.

It had to stop. He was miserable and he hated it. Surely this ache in his chest would eventually go away. He had to start sleeping again, instead of tossing and turning all night, reaching for someone who wasn't there.

Any day now, things would get back to normal. Or at least that's what he kept telling himself.

Lucky for him, he wasn't in love with her, he thought. Then he *really* would be miserable.

He told himself he wasn't staring at her but he couldn't help but notice when Ricky Farraday asked her to dance a few moments later. Ricky was slightly shorter than she was and only fourteen but she took the arm he held out for her with a shake of her head and a laugh he would swear he could hear clear on the other side of the plank dance floor set up in an open area of the garden.

"You're watching those dancers like you'd like to join them."

He jerked his gaze away to realize Frannie had joined him. "No. Not at all. You know I'm not much of a dancer."

"Neither am I. Why don't we trip all over the floor together?"

"I don't think so."

"Come on, Ross. Don't be a big chicken. We haven't

danced together since I was twelve years old on my way to my first junior high school dance and you and Cooper and Flint put on some of Cindy's records and took turns trying to teach me a few steps."

He laughed at the memory of him and his brothers almost coming to blows about who could waltz better. Even though they had bickered their way through it, they had all had a great time that Saturday night. He'd forgotten the whole thing. It was so easy to focus only on the bad times that he often forgot how much fun they could all have together.

"Come on. I'd like to dance," Frannie pressed, showing more enthusiasm about this than she had toward much of anything since her release. How could he say no?

He shrugged. "Don't blame me if I ruin your fancy shoes with my clunky feet."

"I can buy more shoes," she said, and led him out to the dance floor. As he expected, he was rusty and awkward at first but Cindy had passed on at least some small degree of her natural ability and they quickly fell into something resembling dance steps.

The entire time, he was aware of Julie across the dance floor. She laughed at something Ricky said and his heart started to ache all over again.

"Okay, what's wrong?" Frannie asked. "Are you completely miserable to be out here dancing or is something else bothering you?"

He raised an eyebrow, finding her question the height of irony since he'd been hounding her to confide in him about one thing or another since the night her husband was killed.

"Nothing." He could equivocate with the best of them. "I'm just not a huge fan of weddings."

"I love them," she said promptly. "Bethany and Darr look so happy together, don't they?"

He stared at her. "How can you? Love weddings, I mean?"

She gave him an arch look. "Do you think I can't be a romantic, just because my own marriage wasn't the greatest?"

That was just about the biggest understatement of the decade, but he decided to let it slide. "I was thinking more about how tough it would be to love weddings when you grew up with a front-row seat to Cindy's messed-up version of relationships. That's enough to sour anybody on the idea of hearts and flowers and happily-ever-after, don't you think?"

"Oh, Ross." Sorrow flickered in her eyes and her fingers tightened around his. "Don't look to Cindy for an example of anything. Or at me, either."

"You don't think we've inherited her lousy relationship gene?"

"Oh, I hope not. I would hate to think you and Cooper and Flint could never find the same kind of happiness that Darr and Bethany share today."

Against his will, his gaze flickered to Julie, then he looked quickly back at Frannie, hoping she had missed that quick, instinctive look.

"Maybe Cooper and Flint might eventually settle down and you're still a young, beautiful woman," he said. "There's no reason you couldn't find someone someday, someone who will finally treat you like you deserve. But I think at this point, it's safe to say it's not in the cards for me."

She was silent for a long time and he hoped she would let this awkward conversation die. Instead, when her gaze met his, Frannie's eyes were filled with sadness and regret.

"We have all treated you so poorly, haven't we?"

"What do you mean? Of course you haven't!"

"We all counted on you for too much, made you believe you were responsible for everything in our lives. Even Cindy. Maybe especially Cindy."

She squeezed his fingers. "You're not, you know. Not responsible for any of us. You're not responsible for Cindy's failed relationships or her lousy mothering or for my own mistakes or for anything but your own life, Ross, and what you make of it."

So far, he hadn't made much of it. Oh, he had a decent career that he enjoyed and had found success at. But what else did he have to show for forty years on the planet?

"Do you remember teaching me how to ride a two-wheeler without training wheels?" Frannie asked.

He blinked at what seemed an abrupt change of topic. "Not really."

"I do. I can remember it like it was yesterday. I remember exactly what you said to me. I was seven years old, far too old to still be riding a little-kid bike, which means you would have been about eleven. You worked with me for days trying to get me not to wobble. You were so patient, even though I'm sure there were a million other things you would rather have been doing than helping your stupid, clumsy baby sister. Finally one day, you just gave me a big push, let go of the bike frame and told me to forget my fears and just enjoy the ride."

He remembered they had been living in an apartment in Dallas and had gone to the park near their place every afternoon for two weeks. No matter what he tried, Frannie couldn't seem to get the hang of balancing on two wheels. Only after he gave her no other choice except to fall over on the sidewalk did she manage to figure it out. After that, there was no stopping her.

"Can I give the same advice back to you?" Frannie asked, her voice solemn.

"I know how to ride a bike," he muttered, trying to figure out where she was going with this.

"Yes. But do you know how to *live*, Ross?"

He bristled. "What's that supposed to mean?"

"Take it from somebody who feels like she's been one of those ice sculptures over at the bar for the last eighteen years—if a chance for happiness comes along, you have to take it. You can't be afraid because of our messed-up childhood, because of what Cindy did to all of us. Don't give her that much power, Ross. You deserve so much more."

Her words seemed to sear through him, resonating through his entire body. He was doing exactly that. He was still letting Cindy control his life, with her whims and her capriciousness and her instability. He was so convinced he was just like her, that he would mess up everything good and decent that ever came his way, that he was deathly afraid to let go of those fears and take a chance.

Frannie was exactly right. Just as Julie had been right a week before in everything she said to him.

He was afraid to count on anyone else, afraid to open his life to even the possibility of someone else touching his heart.

"I didn't mean to leave you speechless," Frannie said.

He blinked and realized the song had ended—a good thing, since he had stopped stock-still on the edge of the dance floor.

"Think about it, Ross. I just want you to be happy." Frannie kissed his cheek, then slipped away.

The music started up again and somehow Ross managed to make his way off the dance floor before somebody collided with him. He needed a drink, he decided, even if it meant he had to stick around a little longer to give the alcohol time to wear off before he drove home.

Before he could reach the open bar and those ice sculptures Frannie had been talking about, Julie twirled by on the arm of his nephew, who must have asked her to dance the moment Ricky led her off the floor. Her gaze met his over Josh's shoulder and this time he was certain he saw something like sorrow there.

His chest ached again and he had no choice but to rub it as the truth seemed to soak through him.

He couldn't lie to himself anymore. He was in love with Julie Osterman. With her smile and her gentleness and her compassion for everyone around her. He loved the way she touched his arm to make a point and her enthusiasm and dedication to the rough-edged kids she helped and the way she always had everyone else's interests at heart.

He let out a shaky breath, feeling as if a dozen ice sculptures had just collapsed on his head. He *couldn't* be in love with her. He didn't know the first damn thing about being in love.

His instinct was to run, to climb into his SUV and head back to San Antonio, where he was safe. But he had supposedly been safe all week from Julie and these terrifying emotions she churned up in him and he had been miserable.

Just let go and enjoy the ride.

Frannie's words echoed in his mind. Did he have the courage? Could he let go of the past and seize this incredible chance for happiness that had been handed to him?

He watched Julie twirl around the dance floor with Josh and knew he had to try.

Ross was staring at her.

Julie tried to keep her attention on the dance steps, on not tripping all over her partner and making a complete fool of herself, but she was painfully aware of Ross's hard gaze scorching her all over. But why did he bother looking?

He had made it abundantly plain he wasn't interested in anything more than the one night they had together. She had spent all week trying to get over him, to convince herself her heart wasn't broken, and then he had to show up at her friend Bethany's wedding looking rough and masculine and gorgeous in a western-cut dark suit and tie.

If he didn't want her, why was he looking at her like she was a big plate of caramel cashew bars he couldn't wait to gobble up?

She drew in a shaky breath and tried to answer something Josh said, though she wasn't sure if she made any sense. She barely heard what he said in reply, but his next words suddenly penetrated through the haze around her brain.

"What happened between you and Ross?" Josh asked.

She stumbled and nearly stepped on his foot but quickly tried to recover. "What do you mean? Why do you ask?"

His shoulder moved beneath her hand as he shrugged. "I just thought you two were getting along so well. I'm not blind. I could see the vibe between the two of you the night we had dinner. And suddenly it's like you're nowhere to be found and Uncle Ross is acting like a grizzly bear who needs a root canal. What happened between you two?"

She knew it was petty of her to find some satisfaction that Ross was acting cranky but she couldn't seem to help it. "Nothing happened," she lied. Other than they shared one incredible night together and then he broke her heart. "We're just friends."

"Are you sure? He really seemed to like you, more than anyone else I've ever seen him with."

She let out a breath and pasted on something she hoped would pass for a smile. "I'm positive. Just friends."

"Too bad. I think you would have been good for Uncle Ross. He needs somebody like you."

Though she knew Josh didn't realize it, his words poured like acid on her already raw wounds. She was still reeling when the music ended. One of Josh's extended cousins called to him and he excused himself with a smile.

She stood for a moment, aware of Ross across the dance floor talking to his cousin J.R. and J.R.'s lovely fiancée, Isabella Mendoza, who was Roberto's cousin. His gaze met hers one more time, his dark eyes unreadable, and she let out a shaky breath.

Julie couldn't take anymore. She had done her duty by her friend Bethany and had told her how thrilled she was for her and for Darr. There was no reason to stick around for more of this torture.

Quickly, she made her way toward the grassy field that was serving as a parking lot for the wedding, pausing only long enough to say a hasty goodbye to a few friends. Just as she reached the outskirts of the crowd, she heard Ross calling her name.

She briefly entertained the idea of pretending she didn't hear him, but that would be the coward's way out. Besides, as quickly as he moved, he would catch up to her before she could reach her car anyway.

As he approached, she turned slowly, cursing him all over again for making her heart flip in her chest. His features wore an odd, unreadable expression and his eyes were gazing at her with an intensity that made her suddenly breathless.

"Hi, Ross," she managed.

"I thought I saw you leave. I'm glad I caught you. I… needed to talk to you."

"Oh?" She did her best to hide the tremble of her hands by folding them tightly in front of her.

For a long moment, he didn't seem inclined to say anything, he just continued to watch her out of those deep brown eyes. She wasn't used to seeing him at a loss for words and she didn't quite know how to respond.

Finally he let out a long breath. "Do you…would you like to take a walk with me?"

She ought to tell him no. She wasn't at all in the mood to dredge everything up again and she wasn't sure her fragile emotions could handle another encounter with him. But she was curious enough about what he wanted to talk about that she finally nodded. They walked side by side on the gravel pathway around the house in the gathering twilight, through more gardens, their shoulders barely brushing.

The silence between them was jagged, awkward. As a trained therapist, she certainly knew the value of a good silence to allow for thoughts to be gathered, but she couldn't endure this one.

"What did you want to talk to me about?"

He sighed. "I said I *needed* to talk to you. Not that I *wanted* to."

His words stabbed at her already-tender nerves and she stopped abruptly, then turned on her heel and headed back the direction she had come. "Fine," she said over her shoulder. "Let's forget the whole thing. I can find my own way back to my car, thanks all the same."

He grabbed her arm to stop her departure but quickly released her again when she turned back around. "Ah, hell. That didn't come out right. I do want to talk to you."

He was silent for a long moment. When he spoke, his voice was low and rough. "The truth is, I want to do more than talk to you. You're all I've been able to think about for a week."

Her stomach shivered at his words and she folded her arms tightly across it, as if he could see her tremble. "What am I supposed to say to that?"

He looked so uncomfortable that her heart tumbled around all over again in her chest. "I don't know. That maybe you missed me, too."

Only every moment, with every single breath. She swallowed and looked away. "What did you want to talk to me about, Ross? I was just on my way home."

He didn't answer, only started walking again and curiosity gave her no choice but to follow him. He finally stopped near a small, burbling creek that cut through a small copse of trees near one of the outbuildings.

They found a bench there, a weathered iron and wood creation that looked as if it had been there as long as the hills around the ranch. He must have known it was here, she realized, since he had led her directly to this spot. She sat, her emotions in turmoil. After a moment, he sat beside her.

"I love this place," he finally said, his voice low. "It was always my favorite spot whenever we came to the ranch when I was a kid. We didn't do it very often. Come here, I mean. Maybe only two or three times I can remember, but I loved it. I cherished those times because I always felt...*safe* here."

She held her breath, more touched than she knew she ought to be that he had shared this secret place with her, though she still didn't understand why.

He gazed out at the creek, without meeting her gaze. "I didn't feel safe in very many places," he said after another long silence. "You were absolutely right, Julie. Everything you said to me the other morning at your house was right on the money. I keep everyone away because it's easier than letting myself count on people who let me down."

He finally looked at her. "I spent my entire childhood with nothing solid to hold on to but a few fragmented memories of this place."

She couldn't help herself—she reached out to touch his forearm. He looked down at her hand on his sleeve, his eyes deep with emotions she couldn't begin to name, then he covered her hand with his tightly to keep her fingers in place on his arm, to keep the two of them connected.

She could feel the heat of him through the fabric of his suit jacket, feel the muscle tensing beneath her hand. If he found some comfort from her touch, she wasn't about to move.

"My mother should never have had kids," he said hoarsely. "I don't think she wanted any of us and she didn't know what to do with us when we arrived. I was the oldest and it was left to me to take care of everybody else."

"And you did."

"I didn't have a choice. There was no one else. What you said, about keeping everybody out, counting only on myself. You were exactly right. I had to at the time for survival, and it just became a habit, I guess. I denied what you said at first because I didn't want to believe I could be giving my child-hood, my *mother,* that much power to control my life. I'm forty years old. It shouldn't still be so much a part of me."

"We can never completely lose our childhoods," she said softly. "It's part of what shapes us. We just have to learn as adults to accept that we don't have the power to change it. All we can do is try to move forward and make the rest of our lives the best we can."

"You also called me the loneliest man you ever met."

Her eyes stung with tears at the bleakness in his voice. "I'm so sorry, Ross. I should never have said that."

"No. Don't apologize."

He was quiet. In the distance she could hear the music from the wedding, muted and slow. "You were right about that, too," he finally said. "I have been. I never wanted to admit it before. I think I was afraid to face that. I told myself I was perfectly happy, that I liked being on my own, making my own decisions, not having to be responsible for anyone else. But it was only an illusion."

"Oh, Ross."

He let out a shaky breath. "I don't want to be lonely anymore."

Hope fluttered inside her chest like fragile butterfly wings but she was afraid to acknowledge it, afraid to even look at it for fear of crushing it.

He shifted and before she quite realized what he intended, he grabbed both of her hands in his. Her heart began to pound and she couldn't seem to catch her breath.

"This scares the hell out of me," he said, "but I had some good advice thrown back in my face tonight and I'm going to take it. It's time for me to let go of my fears and enjoy the ride."

"I don't know what you're talking about," she murmured. "I'm sorry."

He laughed a little, but his features quickly grew solemn. "I'm in love with you, Julie. That's what I'm talking about."

"What?" Her fingers clenched in his and she would have jerked them away but he held on tightly.

"It's true. I think I've been in love with you probably since you just about whacked me over the head with that silly flowered purse I thought had been stolen."

"You can't be!" The delicate little butterfly of hope inside her became a fierce, joyful dragon, flapping furiously to take flight.

"That's exactly what I've been telling myself for the last week. I've never been in love before. I thought I would get over it, get over you. But seeing you tonight just made me realize this is too big, too deep, for me to just forget about. I can't pretend anymore."

"Ross, I…" her voice faltered and she couldn't seem to string two coherent words together.

"You told me first love was wonderful and terrible at the same time. Do you remember that?"

She nodded, vaguely remembering their conversation about Josh and Lyndsey.

"I've had the terrible part this week, without you. I'm ready for the wonderful part to kick in any time now."

She gazed at him there in the gathering dusk, looking so big and gorgeous and dear. She gave a sound that was half laugh, half sob and crossed the brief distance to throw herself into his waiting arms and press her trembling mouth to his.

He gave an exultant laugh and gripped her tightly, returning her kiss with all the passion and heat and wonder she had dreamed about for the past week.

"I love you, Ross," she murmured against his mouth. "I love you so much. I've been completely miserable this week."

"I probably shouldn't be happy about that, should I? You know what they say about misery loving company."

She laughed. "You could show a little compassion for my suffering."

"That's something you'll have to help me work on. That whole compassion thing you do so well."

"I'll do my best," she promised.

His features grew serious and he drew away a little. "I'm

not the greatest bargain out there, Julie. I can't lie about that. I've still got some things to work through that might take some time. You and I both know you could probably do a whole lot better."

"No, I couldn't. There is no one better." She pressed her mouth to his again and poured every ounce of the love flowing through her into the kiss.

When she drew away, they were both breathing hard. "You are a wonderful man, Ross Fortune. The best man I know. I think I fell in love with you that first night, too, when I saw how concerned you were for everyone else around you but yourself. For Frannie, for Josh. You were even worried about me, and you didn't even know me then. You're good and decent and honorable, Ross. The kind of man a woman knows in her heart will watch out for her and protect her and do everything he can to make her happy."

"You make me want to be all those things and more."

He lifted her until she was sitting on his lap, her arms still wrapped tightly around the strong column of his neck.

"And just so you know," he said, his voice just a whisper against her skin, "you're it for me, Julie. This might be my first time falling in love but it's also my *only* time."

She fought back the sting of tears again and kissed him softly in the pale, lavender light, wondering how she had been blessed enough to love and be loved by two such completely different men.

A tiny part of her heart would always mourn Chris and all the possibilities that had been extinguished too soon. But she was more than ready to move forward, to take this incredible chance she had been given for happiness.

She had a sudden vision of a future with Ross, one that was bright and beautiful and shining with promise. She saw them taking on challenges and causes, opening their lives and their hearts to wounded children, filling their world with joy and laughter. A place where both of them would always feel safe and cherished and loved.

The image was as clear and as real as the huge, round moon beginning to gleam over the treetops. Only this was better.

Worlds better.

As beautiful as it might be, that moon was always just beyond their grasp. But Julie suddenly knew without a doubt that together, she and Ross would grab hold of their future and make it perfect.

* * * * *

"Chief Ranger Rossiter?" The sight of the woman who'd stepped inside Vance's office brought him to his feet. "I'm Rachel Darrow. Your secretary said I should come right in."

"Please," he said, walking around his desk to shake her hand. At a glance he estimated she was in her midtwenties. Her feminine curves did wonders for the pale blue T-shirt and jeans she was wearing. "Ranger Jarvis informed me there's a young boy with you."

The unfriendly expression in her beautiful green eyes caught him off guard. "Yes," was her clipped reply. "When we arrived in Yosemite the ranger told me I couldn't go anywhere in the park until I talked to you first."

"That's right."

"Knowing you wanted this meeting to be private, he offered to show my nephew around Headquarters."

So this woman was the victim's sister.... "What's his name?"

"Nicky."

The boy who haunted Vance's dreams now had a name. "How old is he?"

"He turned six three weeks ago. Were you the man in charge when my brother and sister-in-law were killed?"

"Yes. To tell you I'm sorry for what happened couldn't begin to convey my feelings."

The woman's gaze didn't flicker. "I won't even try to describe mine. Just tell me one thing. Was their accident preventable?"

"Yes," he answered without hesitation.

"In other words, the people working under you fell asleep on your watch and two lives were snuffed out as a result."

Hearing it put like that, he had to set the record straight. "My staff had nothing to do with it. I, myself, could have prevented the loss of life."

Ms. Darrow's expression hardened. "So you admit culpability."

"Yes. I take full blame."

A look of pain crossed over her features. "You can just stand there and admit it?" Her cry echoed that of his own tortured soul.

"Yes." He sucked in his breath.

"I work for a cruise line. Aboard ship, it's the captain's responsibility to maintain rigid safety regulations. If a disaster like that had happened while he was in charge he would have been relieved of his command and never given another ship again."

Rachel Darrow couldn't know she was preaching to the converted. "If you've come to the park with the intention of bringing a lawsuit against me for negligence, maybe you should." It would only be what he deserved.

"Maybe I will."

In the next instant, she wheeled around and hurried out of his office. Vance could have gone after her, but it would cause a scene, something he was loath to do for a variety of reasons. In the first place, he needed to cool down before he approached her again.

The discovery of the Darrows' frozen bodies had affected every ranger in the park. A little boy had been orphaned—a boy whose aunt was all he had left.

* * * * *

Will Rachel allow Vance to explain—and will
she let him into her heart?
Find out in
THE CHIEF RANGER
Available June 2009 from
Harlequin® American Romance®.

We'll be spotlighting a different series every month throughout 2009 to celebrate our 60th anniversary.

Look for Harlequin® American Romance® in June!

Join us for a year-long celebration of the rugged American male! From cops to cowboys— Men Made in America has the hero you've been dreaming about!

Look for

The Chief Ranger

by Rebecca Winters, on sale in June!

Bachelor CEO by Michele Dunaway	July
The Rodeo Rider by Roxann Delaney	August
Doctor Daddy by Jacqueline Diamond	September

You're invited to join our Tell Harlequin Reader Panel!

By joining our new reader panel you will:

- Receive Harlequin® books—they are FREE and yours to keep with no obligation to purchase anything!
- Participate in fun online surveys
- Exchange opinions and ideas with women just like you
- Have a say in our new book ideas and help us publish the best in women's fiction

In addition, you will have a chance to win great prizes and receive special gifts! See Web site for details. Some conditions apply. Space is limited.

To join, visit us at
www.TellHarlequin.com.

REQUEST YOUR FREE BOOKS!

2 FREE NOVELS PLUS 2 FREE GIFTS!

SPECIAL EDITION®

Life, Love and Family!

YES! Please send me 2 FREE Silhouette Special Edition® novels and my 2 FREE gifts (gifts are worth about $10). After receiving them, if I don't wish to receive any more books, I can return the shipping statement marked "cancel." If I don't cancel, I will receive 6 brand-new novels every month and be billed just $4.24 per book in the U.S. or $4.99 per book in Canada. That's a savings of at least 15% off the cover price! It's quite a bargain! Shipping and handling is just 50¢ per book.* I understand that accepting the 2 free books and gifts places me under no obligation to buy anything. I can always return a shipment and cancel at any time. Even if I never buy another book from Silhouette, the two free books and gifts are mine to keep forever.

235 SDN EYN4   335 SDN EYPG

Name	(PLEASE PRINT)

Address	Apt. #

City	State/Prov.	Zip/Postal Code

Signature (if under 18, a parent or guardian must sign)

Mail to the Silhouette Reader Service:
IN U.S.A.: P.O. Box 1867, Buffalo, NY 14240-1867
IN CANADA: P.O. Box 609, Fort Erie, Ontario L2A 5X3

Not valid to current subscribers of Silhouette Special Edition books.

Want to try two free books from another line?
Call 1-800-873-8635 or visit www.morefreebooks.com.

* Terms and prices subject to change without notice. Prices do not include applicable taxes. Sales tax applicable in N.Y. Canadian residents will be charged applicable provincial taxes and GST. Offer not valid in Quebec. This offer is limited to one order per household. All orders subject to approval. Credit or debit balances in a customer's account(s) may be offset by any other outstanding balance owed by or to the customer. Please allow 4 to 6 weeks for delivery. Offer available while quantities last.

Your Privacy: Silhouette is committed to protecting your privacy. Our Privacy Policy is available online at www.eHarlequin.com or upon request from the Reader Service. From time to time we make our lists of customers available to reputable third parties who may have a product or service of interest to you. If you would prefer we not share your name and address, please check here. ☐

SSE09R

**Stay up-to-date
on all your romance
reading news!**

The Inside Romance
newsletter is a **FREE**
quarterly newsletter
highlighting
our upcoming
series releases
and promotions!

Go to
eHarlequin.com/InsideRomance
or e-mail us at
InsideRomance@Harlequin.com
to sign up to receive
your **FREE** newsletter today!

You can also subscribe by writing to us at: HARLEQUIN BOOKS
Attention: Customer Service Department
P.O. Box 9057, Buffalo, NY 14269-9057

Please allow 4-6 weeks for delivery of the first issue by mail.

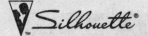

COMING NEXT MONTH

Available May 26, 2009

#1975 A BRAVO'S HONOR—Christine Rimmer
Bravo Family Ties
For more than a century, battling ranch families the Bravos and the Cabreras made the Hatfield and McCoy feud look like child's play. Until Mercy Cabrera fell for Luke Bravo, and their forbidden love tested the very limits of a Bravo's honor.

#1976 A FORTUNE WEDDING—Kristin Hardy
Fortunes of Texas: Return to Red Rock
It had been nearly twenty years since the one-night fling between Frannie Fortune and Roberto Mendoza. But now Roberto was back, and secrets of their past exploded into the present—along with an ironclad love that could not be denied.

#1977 LOVING THE RIGHT BROTHER—Marie Ferrarella
Famous Families
When tragedy struck, Irena Yovich headed back to Hades, Alaska, to console her ex-boyfriend's family—and began seeing his brother Brody Hayes, her best friend from high school, in a very different light. Things were really about to heat up in Hades....

#1978 LEXY'S LITTLE MATCHMAKER—Lynda Sandoval
Return to Troublesome Gulch
When the desperate boy called nine-one-one, little did EMS dispatcher Lexy Cabrera know that the little hero's father, Drew Kimball, whose life they saved that day, would turn around and heal *her*...with a love she'd all but given up on finding!

#1979 THE TYCOON'S PERFECT MATCH—Christine Wenger
The Hawkins Legacy
Brian Hawkins and Marigold Sherwood had spent summers at Hawk's Lake loving each other—until Mari moved away and a misunderstanding tore them apart. Now that CEO Mari was back in town, would all the old feelings come home to roost?

#1980 THE COWBOY'S SECOND CHANCE—Christyne Butler
The Hawkins Legacy
Fate had not been kind to cowboy Landon Cartwright—loss and shame dogged his every step. But then he walked right into the arms of rancher and single mom Maggie Stevens...and a ray of light and love reached the very darkest spots of his soul.